HIGH HURDLE

As I emerged from my breakfast at about seven-thirty in the morning, I heard a huge commotion coming from the centre of the yard. Bret was standing in the middle of the lads, shouting at Charlie, who was in charge of the stables.

"You idiot!" he was yelling. "How could you be so careless?"

Then Bret saw me coming. "And you!" he shouted. "Grudie's your responsibility too! Why do you think I brought you all the way over from England and pay you all this money?"

Charlie tried to intervene.

"And don't try and make excuses!" he roared at him. "You're fired!"

Charlie fired! How could I cope without him? Now we'd never win the race!

GINNY ELLIOT

HIGH HURDLE

Collins

An imprint of HarperCollinsPublishers

To all my godchildren – with love
Nancy Morrison
Mimi Westropp
Sophy Wilson
Camilla Loyd
Peter Coe
Damien Thursby
Freddie Green
George Purbreck

First published in Great Britain by Collins 1997

Collins is an imprint of HarperCollins*Publishers* Ltd,
77-85 Fulham Palace Road, Hammersmith, London W6 8JB.

ISBN 0 00 675164 4

Printed and bound in Great Britain by Caledonian International
Book Manufacturing Ltd, Glasgow, G64

PROLOGUE

It was all Claudia's idea, really. One morning, over coffee in Ned's big warm kitchen, she'd looked up over the rim of her mug, her beautifully varnished nails reflecting the copper and steel around her, flashed her wonderful American smile and said,

"Well, Becky, how about coming over to our wedding in Maryland in the spring?"

I gulped. Of course I knew that Claudia and my grandfather, Ned, were getting married. Ned had met Claudia, a wealthy American widow, on one of his polo-playing trips to the States. But this was the first time that the actual wedding had been mentioned, and my reaction was not very enthusiastic. It was silly, really. I loved Claudia and I knew she cared a lot about me. It's just that I felt – and I hate to admit this – a bit possessive about Ned.

He'd brought me up since I was two years old, when my parents had been killed in a car accident, and he'd looked after me and encouraged me all my life. I knew I wouldn't really be losing him, but I just didn't feel all that great about kissing him goodbye, either.

"Well—" I stammered.

"You'll have a great time and Ned and I are desperate to have you there – it's such a special day. And wait till you meet Pammy, my niece – she's something else!"

"OK, Claudia," I said, hoping I didn't sound too ungracious, "that sounds great, but when's it going to be? You know there's a couple of big races coming up and—"

"I know, I know," said Claudia, tossing back her sleek blonde hair, "but I've got it all worked out. Ned and I will go over ahead of you – I need to organise the preparations – and then you can follow us after the races are over." And she gave me one of her big, scented hugs.

And that was how it all began. Claudia, who knows everyone who's anyone in the States, had a very old friend called Dick Mann, who'd been killed recently in a car accident. Well, his son, Charlie, was working as an assistant trainer at one of the top stables, owned by a super-rich guy called Bret King, who was a bit of a firebrand, she said.

It appeared that Claudia, in her usual over-the-top way, had been singing my praises to Bret King, particularly about my work with horses who'd had some tricky problems. Apparently, she'd been so convincing that she'd persuaded him I could really help with Grudie, one of his top horses, who needed some special handling. The trainer at his own yard had been unable to straighten out his bad habits with any conventional methods.

So now Claudia had got me invited over there to train Grudie for the Maryland Hunt Cup – one of America's most important races (and the most thrilling!). And here I was, on my way to the airport, to fly out with Paddy (my all-time favourite horse) to the States. Paddy was going to run in the Hunt Cup, too, while I trained this (apparently) amazing horse, Grudie.

Charlie Mann had already faxed me with all the details about Grudie's form, his looks, his breeding – and, more to the point, his problems. And I had agreed to go over and sort them out!

I'd thought it would be more difficult for me to get time away from the Mainwarings' stables, where I worked, but Ben and Sue had been wonderful, too. Ben had made a joke about his "jet-setting assistant trainer" but I could tell he was really pleased for me. And Sue, always big-hearted, had put her arm round me and promised that everything would run like clockwork in my absence.

I'd said goodbye to Scruffy and Shelley, our two dogs, had a farewell party with the lads at the stables, packed my bags and was ready for off. Little did I know that I was about to be drawn into one of the biggest dramas of my life. Here I was, seventeen, and about to embark on a new adventure!

CHAPTER ONE

The mini-cab deposited me at the airport and I suddenly felt quite small and alone, but then I remembered Paddy, who would be nervous and sweating if I didn't get to him soon. The horsebox had come for him early that morning and he'd gone off with John and Jessie, two of the best lads, to look after him. It's not that I didn't trust them, it's just I have a special relationship with Paddy and I knew that, right then, he needed me.

I checked my baggage in and was quickly directed to the gate for the horses' departure building. It led into a vast hangar where the horseboxes were waiting, ready to be lifted up and deposited into the wide body of the aircraft. I looked around for the special groom that horses are allocated when flying – someone who understands horses and knows exactly what to do if there's any kind of problem on the journey. I spotted Mick at once – I'd travelled with him several times before, when I'd taken horses out to race in Ireland. He was brilliant, someone who had the knack of making both horses and trainers feel relaxed.

As I walked towards him, he turned and gave me a friendly wave.

"Hi, Becky," he said, cheerily. "So we've got the big ugly brute travelling today, have we?"

He always teases me about Paddy's Pet. Paddy's a big horse with a huge head – no oil painting, really, which reminds me... But no, I mustn't get distracted!

I walked up the ramp of the horsebox to check on Paddy, who nudged my shoulder and whinnied and tried to stand on my foot in his usual friendly way! I suddenly felt relieved to be standing next to him – his familiar smell made me feel less daunted by the thought of what lay ahead. I stroked his neck and, at a nod from Mick, went out of the hangar towards the big, fat, looming belly of the aircraft.

I was really relieved that Mick was with us. As the plane took off, the noise of the engine's thrust sent the horses into a panic and Mick quickly led us into a round of singing. This helps to drown out the engine noise and lessens the disorientation that horses always feel on take-off and helps to calm them down. Not that my voice is anything to write home about, but I found myself singing *Danny Boy* and other Irish tunes at the top of my lungs, and it certainly seemed to work.

Our ten-hour flight was uneventful. Mick kept on checking the horses and talked to them almost constantly in his quiet, lilting voice. In between times we chatted, and talking to Mick made me realise just how much I was looking forward to my new job, even though I felt terrified out of my skin at the same time.

Mick was really helpful, telling me the skills the horses needed to jump the fixed fences in the Hunt Cup, and how it took a big-hearted horse even to attempt their huge size. He made me feel very proud of Paddy when he said, "Sure, he'll manage it fine, that horse of yours.

With a bit of extra training out there and some practice over similar fences, he'll knock the socks off those Yankee horses!"

But I still had to pinch myself when we started singing at the tops of our voices again as the aircraft began its descent. I sang so loudly my ears felt numb and my heart started to pound excitedly as I saw the skyline of Baltimore airport coming into view. I was really here! Me, Becky, in the States, coming to train a horse for one of the most famous races in the country!

As I was watching the horseboxes being unloaded at the airport, a voice at my shoulder said, "Excuse me. Are you Becky?"

I turned to find myself staring into the bluest eyes I'd ever seen. I nodded, dumbly.

"Hi, I'm Charlie Mann, Bret King's assistant trainer. Welcome to Maryland."

So this was Charlie! I wondered how he viewed my arrival here – after all, normally he'd be the one training Grudie.

I stepped back and found myself looking up at him, taking in all the vital details. He was slim and tanned, with a rangy physique and he was looking at me with a quiet intelligence which I have to admit I found immediately attractive. The blue of his eyes was enhanced by a faded denim jacket worn over a checked shirt, and he had on jeans and brown boots.

"Oh, hi," I managed to say at last. "I'm really glad you're here. We were just wondering what to do next."

"We'll get the horsebox over to my truck and I'll take you both to your new home," he said, smiling.

Mick was busy hitching the goose neck to the airport truck, and Charlie and I went over and got into the cab beside the driver. As we made our way over to the checkpoint (we had loads of papers for Paddy, as well as my ticket and passport) I waved goodbye out of the window at Mick, who yelled, "You show 'em, Becky!" much to my embarrassment. But Charlie just smiled slightly as I turned back to him, suddenly hit by a wave of tiredness.

As if he could sense this, Charlie said, "I guess you must be feeling a bit exhausted right now. When we get to the stables, we'll find someone to settle Paddy and I'll show you to your quarters right away – we can talk when you've had a chance to rest a bit, OK?"

"OK," I said gratefully, leaning back against the seat, and gradually, as we left the urban complex of the airport, I began to take in my surroundings. The afternoon was bright with a clear blue sky and I could feel the warmth of the early spring sunshine through the windscreen. I was struck by the beautiful trees everywhere, just beginning to come into bud (much earlier than back home, where winter still seemed to be in full swing).

The countryside was open and quite flat with pretty, clapboard houses and farms here and there, each with its own white-painted picket fences. They reminded me of films I'd seen, and I felt a thrill of excitement and anticipation as we drove towards Bret's place.

"Tell me a bit about yourself," said Charlie, "that is, if you're not too tired."

Well, I do have this tendency to gabble when I'm tired or nervous, and I was both! So poor Charlie got the whole works. I told him all about Claudia and Ned getting married and

about Red Rag and Paddy and the
Mainwarings and Scruffy and Shelley and the
lads and suddenly realised I'd been talking too
much and was forgetting my manners.

"Can you fill me in on Bret King?" I asked
him politely. "He sounds pretty alarming,
from what Claudia told me."

"Sure," he said, and for the first time I
noticed his lean, tanned hands on the steering
wheel. "First of all," he began, "he's a big man
– big in all senses of the word. He's large and
loud and red-haired, and you sure know when
he's around. He was dirt poor to begin with
and made his fortune out of buying a piece of
scrub land that turned out to have oil under it
like you wouldn't believe."

Charlie sounded as though he had some
admiration for Bret, though I noticed he was
trying to keep his voice free of any emotion.
He went on. "Now he makes his money out of
real estate deals. It seems to be important to
him who he knows, especially in the real estate
business, and he likes people to know him. He
needs good connections – but most of all, he
likes success, and the success of his yard and

his horses is everything to him. It represents a sign to all those well-heeled, Ivy-League, old-money folks that he, Bret King, has made it – big time!"

"He's got a son, hasn't he?" I asked. Claudia had mentioned one.

"Yeah," said Charlie, with a rueful grin. "Rick. He's not bad, just a bit of a spoiled brat sometimes, but we used to be good friends, still are, really . . ." his voice trailed off.

"And *your* father – Dick? Claudia said he was killed recently, in a car accident."

Why do I do that? As soon as a thought comes into my mind, it jumps out. At least, when I'm nervous it does. As soon as I asked Charlie about his father, I could sense that it was the wrong thing to have said. Charlie's face froze a little and his hands gripped the wheel a bit tighter.

"Look, sorry," I muttered, "I shouldn't have asked that."

"That's OK," he said, relaxing slightly. "It's all just a bit too recent for me to be able to talk about yet, that's all."

"I understand," I said, smiling at his profile.

And as I looked round and out of the window again, I saw white picket fences stretched along the drive as it curved round towards the biggest spread I had ever seen in my life. I had finally arrived at Bret King's Racing Stables.

CHAPTER TWO

As I jumped down from the truck, a barrage of flashlights popped in my face. I blinked and stepped back, surprised. There was a knot of journalists and photographers grouped together in the yard, and all looking at me!

I was staggered. Charlie came round the side of the jeep and put his hand gently under my elbow, steering me towards them.

"The local press have heard about your arrival, Becky, and they're here to welcome you to Maryland," he said, smiling down at me. One of the journalists stepped forward.

"Hi, Becky," he said, holding out his hand. "I'm Dan Ricardo, I'm doing a feature on you and Mr King's stables for *Pacemaker* magazine. Mr King's given me free range around the place for a couple weeks."

I looked at him as I shook his hand, taking in a tall, dark, young man in his late twenties. He looked sort of "cute" as the Americans would say, but had very astute brown eyes. He was wearing preppy clothes – chinos and a jacket, with a stripy tie and a button-down shirt.

"OK," said Charlie, guiding me past Dan Ricardo and the others. "Just one more picture, and that's all for now." Other journalists were pressing in towards me and thrusting microphones under my nose, calling out questions.

"Becky's real tired and needs to get herself and her horse settled after the long flight," Charlie said, smiling but determined as he addressed the waiting throng.

The cameras popped again and as I turned and smiled, Dan Ricardo called out, "I'll talk to you later, Becky, if that's OK? When you've rested." I watched as he turned and went over to a car. I have to admit, I liked the look of Dan Ricardo. There was definitely something interesting about him.

Charlie led me through the Barn, as these huge stables are called in America. Perhaps because they were covered by a vast, barn-like construction, protecting them from extremes of weather – in this part of the world, the heat of a Maryland summer and the below-zero temperatures and snow in the winter.

I was truly amazed! They were the most sumptuous stables I had ever seen! Even the most prestigious yards in England didn't look like these. The cobbled floor was gleaming with not a speck of dirt in sight and the wooden stables shone in the sunlight, stretching a long way through the Barn, and there wasn't a speck of straw or hay or muck anywhere to be seen.

Charlie led me over to another group of people.

"Becky, meet your fellow companions, the stable lads," he said, as he guided me over to a relaxed and friendly-looking bunch of young people. They were wearing baseball hats with "Bret King's Racing Stables" written across the front of them, and jeans and trainers. They looked as clean as the horses and as fit. I began to wonder just how the Americans did it, thinking fondly of Jessie and John and the other lads back home in their motley collection of gear.

"Hi, Becky!" they chorused.

"Hi," I replied, and Charlie began to introduce me. Just as he'd finished saying, "and this is Scott, Kelly and Karen," another voice broke in:

"Well, Charlie, aren't you going to introduce me to the little lady?"

I guessed immediately. It had to be Rick.

And I was right. Out of the corner of my eye, I'd spotted Rick watching us from where he'd been standing on the edge of the crowd, casually leaning against one of the stable doors. Now he strolled rather arrogantly towards us, limping slightly, I noticed, but looking every inch the boss's son. He was wearing too-tight cord trousers and an expensive-looking leather jacket over a green silk shirt. His trousers were tucked into black leather boots and a Rolex watch hung loosely on his wrist. I shivered slightly.

"Sure," said Charlie. "Becky, this is Rick

King. Rick, this is Becky, all the way from England and right now, in need of a rest."

"Well," drawled Rick, eyeing me up and down, "a pleasure to meet you, a real pleasure."

I felt a sudden rush of anger at his lazy appraisal of me. "Hi, Rick," I said, "sorry to rush off, but Charlie's right, I'm really tired suddenly, but maybe we could get together tomorrow?"

I could sense Rick felt I'd brushed him off, but I couldn't help it. I just wanted to get to my room and be on my own for a bit.

Charlie led me through the rest of the yard, pausing to take in the office and to point out the computer, where the details of all the horses were kept. I just couldn't get over how clean and orderly everything appeared – right down to the little kitchen the lads used and the magnificent tack room. Right at the end of a double row of stables stood the lads' quarters, looking like a small ranch house itself. This was where my room would be too, and Charlie, carrying my bags, led me over to the stairs running up the outside of the building to the first floor. We walked up together and at the top, Charlie turned to me and pointed past the Barn to the countryside beyond.

"That's where Bret and Rick live," said Charlie.

Next to the vast spread of Bret's stables stood his own ranch-style house. It was incredible. I'd only seen houses as grand as that in TV programmes like *Dallas* and it was hard to believe this one was real. It was built in the shape of an E, and it sat low and luxurious in its beautifully tended gardens, a blue pool nearby glinting in the sunshine. The drive from the Barn over to the ranchhouse was tarmac and had lights all the way down it, making the place look like an expensive golf club. Not quite my taste, but still pretty amazing. What would Ben and Sue think of this, I wondered, suddenly feeling a pang of homesickness.

As if sensing this, Charlie turned to me.

"I'll leave you now, Becky. I'll just carry your bags in and show you your room. We can meet up tomorrow and I'll introduce you to your most important companion – Grudie. I'll bet he's champing at the bit to meet you."

I grinned at him as we turned and went into the lads' sleeping quarters. We walked through a sitting-room, with a large TV and CD player and comfortable sofas and chairs, into a long corridor with rooms off either side. At the far end there was a door which said ASSISTANT TRAINER. Charlie explained that this was my room and that if he hadn't lived so close, this is where he would be living.

He pushed open the door and my mouth dropped open. I don't quite know what I'd expected, but this looked like a five-star hotel room. There was a huge bed and a walk-in cupboard and a whopping great TV in the corner of the room. There was a little fridge and a desk with writing paper and pens and a comfortable chair. Charlie dumped my bags on a luggage rack at the end of the bed and walked over to another door.

"This is your bathroom, Becky," he said, pushing it open.

"Wow!" is all I managed to breathe at him and he grinned, glad that I looked pleased.

"I'll leave you to it, then," he said, pausing briefly to flash me a look from those amazing blue eyes. Then he raised his hand and left.

I looked around me. It was all wonderful. On one side of the room was a long window with views across the countryside and a small balcony with a wooden chair and table outside to sit at on warm summer evenings. I slid open the window and breathed deeply. It was strange how air really did smell different in other countries. As I turned back into my room, I suddenly thought of Jamie and how we'd have giggled at the luxury of it all if we'd been there together.

Jamie was my boyfriend. At least, we'd been together for the past year, but he was a top National Hunt jockey and with our busy lives, we were both trying not to get too serious. He was gorgeous, and I suddenly thought of his dark hair falling over his handsome face, and his blue eyes smiling at me. I walked across to the desk and rummaged around for a post card to send to him. I pulled it towards me and began writing:

> Jamie
> I'm here at last! You wouldn't believe this place, it's like something out of 'Dallas'. My room is huge and the Barn is so clean you could eat off the floor – even the horses look shiny! I've met Charlie (nice) and Rick (slimy) but not Mr Big (Bret King) or Grudie. About to go and check on Paddy. Lads look friendly. Miss you lots, and Scruffy and the lads.
> > Hugs and kisses,
> > Becks

I felt better when I'd written it but still rather small and far from home, so I decided to go and visit Paddy to see how he'd settled in to his quarters. Pulling my bedroom door shut behind me, I ran down the steps to the stables where I spotted one of the lads, Kelly, and asked her where they'd stabled Paddy.

"He's right over here," she said, pointing to the first stable on the right, "real close to your room. We figured you and he would like to be near each other," she grinned.

I nodded and smiled at her as I walked to his stable. I looked over the door and there he was, his huge, dear familiar head bent towards his hay basket. He sensed my presence immediately and flung up his head, turning to walk towards me.

"Oh, Paddy," I murmured into his neck, his familiar smell making me feel homesick all over again. Tears began to slide slowly down my cheeks and into his coat as I stroked him, thinking of everyone we'd left behind and everything I had to do here.

I sniffed loudly, suddenly aware just how silly I would look if someone saw me sobbing into my horse's neck, feeling sorry for myself. "Listen, Paddy," I said out loud, "I'm going to do the best job I've ever done here and I'm going to make Ned and Claudia really proud of me, and you, too, you funny old horse!"

Paddy whinnied again and I gave him a

final pat and turned back towards my room
and the new life that lay ahead of me.

CHAPTER THREE

In spite of all the new sensations flooding my head, I slept like a log, only waking to the sound of the lads banging about in their rooms nearby. I stretched luxuriously in my wonderful bed and saw bright sun filtering through the thick curtains at my window.

Right, Becky, I told myself, this is the start of your new life, and you'd better be impressive.

A quiet tap on my door made me jump out of bed.

"Come in," I called brightly.

"Becky, hi, good morning." It was Kelly. "Charlie suggested I give you a wake-up call, he thought you might be jet-lagged."

"Thanks, Kelly. He was right. I slept like a

29

log. Do we get breakfast downstairs in that kitchen I spotted?"

"Yeah," she said. "We all grab what we want. There're English muffins, toast, juice – anything you want, really. And coffee, there's always a pot of coffee ready to go," she grinned.

"I'll be right down," I said. "Tell Charlie I'll see him in fifteen minutes."

I dressed and hurried along to the kitchen, where I saw Charlie bending over the huge shiny toaster, pulling out some muffins.

"Charlie, good morning," I said to his back. As he turned round, smiling, I was struck again by how good looking he was.

"Hi, Becky. Did you sleep OK?" he asked. "Yeah," he said, seeing me eye his breakfast, "I like to eat over here, with the lads. It gives me a chance to go over the daily routines with everyone. Plus, Bret likes to see me first thing – to hear what's happening that day."

I could feel my stomach tighten again. Bret King. I'd heard so much about him I was beginning to feel terrified.

"I'll take you up to the house when you've

had your breakfast," said Charlie. "Now, what would you like? Let me do the honours today."

When we'd had breakfast and chatted about the daily routines – the computerised training programmes for each horse which Charlie always typed in the night before, and the daily feeding programmes – we made our way outside to the yard's golf buggy.

"This is what we ride in up to Bret's place," said Charlie, smiling at my expression of surprise. "It saves time in a place this size," he added, "and Bret's hot on that. 'Time is money' is one of his favourite sayings."

We climbed in the buggy and cruised out of the yard towards the winding drive I'd seen from the stairs the night before. I suddenly thought of Ned and Claudia and their wedding at the weekend and hoped the weather would stay fine. Claudia was planning to have the ceremony in her sister's home and most of it was to be outside.

I broke out of my daydream to concentrate on what Charlie was saying to me.

"Don't be alarmed by Bret, Becky," he said.

"He's noisy and big but he's backing you all the way. But he likes to win, so he's going to make darned sure that you take Grudie to the Hunt Cup and walk away with first prize."

Charlie swung the buggy up to the front door and jumped out. As he came round to my side, the house door opened and a maid in a frilly white apron appeared.

"Morning, Mr Charlie," she smiled. "It's sure a pretty one. Mr King's waiting for you on the terrace."

"Morning, Charlotte. This is Becky, she's over here from England to train one of Mr King's horses for the Hunt Cup."

"Morning, Miss Becky," she said, looking at me with friendly curiosity. She held open the door and we walked through a marbled hallway towards huge glass doors which opened on to a patio and the garden beyond.

As we stepped through the doors into the morning sunshine once again, a tall man heaved himself up from a chair and strode towards us with his hand held out to me.

"Ah, Becky," he said, "at last. Welcome to Maryland. Hope you've settled in OK and that

Charlie here is taking care of you." That was obviously as much as Mr Bret King could manage when it came to niceties – without waiting for an answer, he went on: "Now, let's get down to business."

He was certainly a big guy, easily six foot six, with flaming red hair. He looked powerful standing there in his business suit, as though he was used to having people jump when he said so. But his glance was mean and knowing as he shook my hand, and I didn't like the way he eyed me up and down. This was the kind of man I was instinctively wary of. But I mentally shook myself and walked with him and Charlie towards the table.

"Take a seat both of you. Coffee, Becky? Here, help yourself."

Charlie poured us both a cup of coffee and shot me a reassuring look.

"First, let's talk about Grudie," said Bret, turning to face me. "He's a real big-hearted horse – one helluva horse, in fact, and he jumps like a dream. He's small but he's intelligent and he's got guts. Trouble is, he's a bit too full of himself and he makes mistakes. He's fallen a couple times because he's impetuous, but once you win him over, you should have no problem with him." This was more or less what I'd heard before, but the next sentence gave more clues to Bret himself. "He's got stamina and loyalty – he's a horse in a million – and I *want that Cup*."

Phew! So there it was. All Bret's aspirations and desires were bound up in this one horse. It would really make Bret's reputation as a racing stable owner if Grudie could win this Cup, with the most prestigious people in America watching. I could see that now.

"I can't wait to meet Grudie, Mr King," I said. "I'm really looking forward to working with him – I just want to get started."

"That's what I like to hear," said Bret. "Though I have to say, I was surprised to see you're so . . . well, so young," he added. "But I've been told that, for a girl, you're strong and have a real way with horses."

I decided to ignore his sexist attitude. I'd met people like Bret before and the only way to change their attitudes towards women was to prove just how good you were, and that's exactly what I intended to do.

"You'll be working under my trainer, Max Shand," Bret went on. "He's the best, but he has to go across to Connecticut to a major horse sale at the end of this week, so you'd better make the most of your time with him before that. When he's gone, Charlie's in charge. And make sure you do a good job, ya hear?" he said, swinging round in his chair to face Charlie, who looked faintly startled at this attack.

"OK. That's it," Bret went on, not wasting any more time. "I'll be down to the yard first thing tomorrow morning to make sure everything's going according to plan."

He swung round and strode back into the house. We heard him yelling for Rick as we got up ourselves and walked into the house together, with me gazing round in fascination. Everything was way over the top and there was not a shred of good taste in sight. Gilt and marble were everywhere, and the bookshelves looked as though the books had been ordered by the metre. Thick fur rugs littered the floor and a huge bar dominated one corner.

As we walked into the hallway, we met Rick leaving what was obviously Bret's study – I caught a glimpse of dark red walls, more books and green and gold lamps through the door. Rick looked like thunder as he pulled the door shut behind him.

"Morning, Rick," said Charlie.

Rick grunted a greeting but as he turned to me he had a smarmy smile on his face. "Ah, ha, Becky. Good morning. I trust you slept well," he said, eyeing me up and down again in that slimy way he had. Angry, I could feel my face blushing.

"Fine, thanks, Rick," I said, turning to leave. Rick followed us through the main door and out to the buggy.

"I guess I'll just hitch a ride with you guys over to the yard," he said. "I'm sure Becky won't mind making room for me, will you, Becky?"

I'd rather sit with a snake, I thought to myself. But still, he was the boss's son and it would be crazy to fall out with him at this early stage. I climbed into the buggy next to Charlie, and Rick swung himself up, making a point of leaning against me and putting his free arm along the back of my seat. I really did not like being that close to him!

Somehow I knew that Charlie sensed my feelings, and he turned towards me, giving me another reassuring smile.

"This is Grudie," said Charlie.

We'd just walked through the line of stables, pausing to say hello to Paddy on the way. He was being groomed till he gleamed by Kelly, who'd clearly taken a liking to him. He'd whickered in happy recognition and, satisfied that he was fine, we'd moved on down the yard towards Grudie.

Now I found myself looking at the large ugly head of a chestnut horse. Charlie walked across to the stable door and patted his neck.

"Hey, Grudie, this is Becky, your new trainer, and you're gonna learn to do exactly what she tells you," he whispered. I could see that Charlie had a real affinity with horses as Grudie tossed his head up and down, snorting through his nostrils and butting Charlie gently on the shoulder.

"Come into the stable and you can take a good look at him," said Charlie, not noticing my glum expression.

To be honest, my heart had sunk. Grudie was just not what I'd expected. I thought he'd be bigger and more elegant, like the prime steeplechasers in England. But this horse was small! I began to wonder what on earth I was doing in this place, far from home, working for a man I didn't like the look of, with a son who was a real slimeball. And now this! Grudie was like the Ugly Duckling!

Charlie was opening the half-door of the stable and Grudie began to look excited, tossing his big head up and down again in anticipation.

I walked quietly into the stable with Charlie in front of me.

"Hi, Grudie," I said, putting my hand on his neck, and stroking it down towards his forelegs. I looked at him carefully, taking in his unusual chestnut colouring and mane with flaxen streaks in it, down the length of his long body and athletic hind quarters. Although his legs were short, they were strong limbs. My impression of Grudie, now I was close to him, was one of immense power.

He moved nervously around me, like a coiled spring, and I could see exactly what Charlie had meant when he'd told me that Grudie was highly-strung and exuberant. I was going to have to get to know this horse really well. My heart sank even further.

"I'll leave you two together for a while, Becky. When you're ready, come on over to the office and I'll show you the set-up. Max isn't around today, he's gone to give advice to a neighbour who's having a bit of trouble with one of his mares. But he'll be here tomorrow."

I spent some time with Grudie, talking to him and getting to know him – taking in his shape and strength. When I felt I'd seen enough for one day, I let myself out of his stable and headed off to Paddy.

As I approached his stable, and saw his familiar shape, I felt a rush of homesickness once more. I really wanted this job to work out, but I just didn't know if I'd be up to it. The only bright thing on the horizon was Charlie, but he wouldn't be around all the time. And what about Max Shand? If I liked him as much as I liked Bret, I really would be in for a bad time. I began to kick myself for letting Claudia persuade me to come. Oh, Ned! I suddenly thought of him and longed to be able to talk to him and tell him everything I'd seen. Even though it wouldn't be long till I saw him at the wedding, I knew I'd be lucky if Claudia let me get a word in edgeways!

As I rounded the corner of the stable block, I caught sight of Dan Ricardo, the journalist who'd been waiting to see me when I'd arrived at the yard. That all seemed a long time ago, even though it was only yesterday. He saw me and raised his hand in greeting, but made no attempt to come over and chat to me. My mind still caught up with Ned and Grudie, it wasn't till later that I thought his behaviour was odd. Hadn't he wanted to interview me? But he simply closed the office door and walked off towards the ranch house.

When I went to bed that night, my head was aching with all the new things I'd taken in that day. Charlie – helpful and caring, (and, I had to admit, pretty delicious), Bret, Rick, the stable lads, the hi-tech office with its computerised training and feeding routines for each horse, the gleaming stables running like clockwork and Grudie, the ugly, small, strong, jumpy horse I'd come to train. But what if I failed? I shivered and sank down into my comfortable bed, pulling the duvet over my head and hoping everything would look better in the morning.

CHAPTER FOUR

After another breakfast of muffins, bacon and coffee, Charlie said that he wanted to introduce me to Max, who had his own small office next to the main one. He led me through the yard and, right outside the door, I saw a small, wiry man, chatting to Scott, one of the lads.

As we walked towards him, he turned. I noticed shrewd grey eyes in a weather-beaten face and, quite suddenly, felt much more confident. I knew from Charlie that Max had been born and brought up in Maryland and had been a brilliant jockey himself and somehow, when I saw him, I could sense that here was someone who really knew everything there was to know about horses – the kind of person I was used to dealing with.

He was wearing jodhpurs and a checked shirt with a padded body-warmer over the top. He had a tweed cap pulled low over his dark curly hair, which was beginning to go grey at the temples. His riding boots shone in the morning sunshine.

"Well now, you must be Becky," he said, shaking my hand with his firm, dry, gnarled one. "I hear you had some time with Grudie yesterday, and I bet you just can't wait to try him out." He steered me towards the tack room.

"Let's get you kitted out and then you and I'll go out on the track, to test out our friend."

The tack room, which I'd only looked into briefly the day before, was another surprise. Unlike the Mainwarings' warm, scruffy one, with cats and dogs lying about on horse blankets, this one was pristine. The wood-clad walls gleamed with the sheen of dark mahogany and mounted all around the room were paintings and photographs of the horses and the races they'd been in. Carefully arranged, as if in the smartest American department store, was an array of shelves, each labelled with the names of the horses and stable personnel. Max led me over to the shelf named "Grudie" and showed me where his tack would normally be.

"Scott's already saddled him up, but this is his slot," he said, "and right over here is yours." He showed me a shelf with my name already marked beneath it in green, yellow and white, the stable colours.

"Here's your kit, Becky." He smiled, seeing my surprise. "We pride ourselves on efficiency here," he said, pulling down a whip and a riding hat. "I hope we made the right guess at your size."

I pulled on the hat and found it fitted perfectly! Did this yard ever do anything wrong?

"Anything else you need, just ask Kelly," said Max, looking pleased. "Now, let's get going."

As I mounted Grudie, I could feel his power beneath me. His body tensed in anticipation of the ride to come and his ears twitched incessantly. I soon came to learn that he did this when he was anxious and excited. Although he wasn't the horse of my dreams, I found I was beginning to like him. He looked alert and intelligent as we walked out of the yard towards the track.

I felt the warmth of the early spring sunshine on my back and smelt the fresh Maryland air as Max and I began to trot up the slope. Max was riding Jupiter, a big, heavy horse with a long stride. He told me that Jupiter had a calming influence on Grudie and that's why he always rode them together on training sessions.

"Becky, I want you to give him his head when you get to the top. Follow the course and, if you want to, take that fence mid-way through. See how you feel!" he called.

I could feel Grudie all right. I also felt pretty anxious, I can tell you, and I sensed that Max would never really have confidence in me until I'd proved myself with Grudie. I saw, way over in the distance, a typical Hunt Cup timber fence, with fixed post and rails. I'd read up all about the race, which was traditionally run over huge timber fences, some four bars and some five bars high, and I knew that any horse that jumped them had to have real guts.

I leaned forward and Grudie, as if started by a pistol, sprang into action. I could feel his fantastic energy and enthusiasm through the saddle. His ears twitched like crazy and his bottom lip began to flap up and down – another of his funny habits, which later I got to know well. He always did this when he was excited.

We galloped round the course, getting the feel of each other, but I sensed that Grudie had his eyes already set on the fence in the distance. He wanted to jump it. Grudie was obviously just one of those horses who liked a challenge, and I was going to have to take it on! He was beginning to pull hard, eager to get away from me and do his own thing. I had to use all my riding skills to keep him checked, but at the same time I knew he was one of the most thrilling rides I'd ever experienced. My excitement was infecting Grudie even more and I knew that this first ride together was a potentially explosive one.

OK, Becky, here goes, I said to myself. I

knew Grudie had to jump that fence, and I knew that I had to, as well, if Max was going to have any confidence in me. I kept Grudie on a straight course as we thundered over the ground. Somehow I managed to calm my nerves, knowing how highly-strung Grudie was, and realising that I just had to keep my body as still as possible if we were going to get over this high fence in one piece.

As we got nearer the timber jump, Grudie seemed to fly over the ground, his stride beginning to lengthen in anticipation. I was going to have a hard job pacing him for this – he was so impetuous – and I certainly didn't want to fall! My heart was thumping hard in my chest as we closed on the fence. And then we were there. Grudie's strong hind quarters pushed us up, up and he curled his forelegs high under his chest as we sailed over the jump. It seemed to take us for ever to arch down the other side, but we landed safely and I'd managed to sit still and calm as we'd made the jump. Luckily, I didn't fall in a heap on his neck, so we were able to gallop on round the rest of the course.

As we thundered up to Max on our return, I felt exhilarated. Grudie might not look beautiful, but I knew then that he was a horse in a million. His superb energy and intelligence just shot us over the jump, but there was one thing I had learnt: somehow I would have to control his impetuous nature. There was no way that a jockey could avoid complete disaster if Grudie ran the whole course on super-charge, the way he'd just done over the gallops. But I knew in my heart that he had what it took to be a winner.

I slowed to a canter and then trotted up to Max. I could feel my skin glowing with pleasure and a stupid grin seemed to have got stuck on my face. Max looked pleased, too.

"Well, now, Becky," he said, as I reined in next to Jupiter. "You sure handled that well. I knew just what Grudie wanted to do, but I didn't know if you were gonna feel the same! I guess you could sense how crazy he is to jump and you're just gonna have to find a way of keeping his enthusiasm under control, but let his stamina and energy win through at the end. Think you can do it?"

"Sure," I nodded, out of breath. "He's a fantastic horse, Max. I know he could win the Cup. I'm just going to try and teach him a few tricks about timing. That way he should be able to use his talent and strength to the full – not blow it all in the first few fences." I was eager to let Max know what had been racing through my mind.

As we rode back, chatting, to Bret's yard, I shot a look at Max from under the brim of my hat. He looked quietly happy and confident and I let out a huge sigh of relief. I knew I could do it. I knew I could win that Cup for Bret King now, and I just couldn't wait to get started.

But as we rode into the yard and I kicked my feet out of the stirrups, I glimpsed that reporter again. He was running down the steps leading from the living quarters and when he saw us he disappeared rapidly round the corner of the tack-room block. What was he doing? I knew he'd wanted to speak to me again, but his behaviour was starting to look pretty fishy. I made a mental note to talk to Charlie about him.

CHAPTER FIVE

The wedding! The day dawned bright and sunny, with only a few high clouds scudding across the big blue Maryland sky. For some reason I woke up quite nervous, but it was probably just because I was worried about losing Ned.

Claudia, with her usual sense of occasion, had given me a wonderful dress to wear. As I jumped out of bed, I couldn't wait to put it on – a great change from my usual jeans and jodhpurs! Secretly, I wondered what Charlie would think of me when he collected me in the pick-up which was to pull Paddy's horse trailer.

Yes, that was my big surprise wedding present for Ned and Claudia! I was going to lead Paddy, groomed to the hilt, up the red carpet in the marquee. He was going to be wearing an oil painting hung on a red satin ribbon round his neck. I'd had the painting specially commissioned from a friend of mine, who was an artist and a jockey. She'd copied a photograph of Ned, Claudia, me and Paddy, and I just couldn't wait to see their faces. Imagine Paddy, the horse they both adored, arriving at their wedding with this fantastic portrait as well. I felt very pleased with myself for thinking of such a brilliant idea.

I showered and made myself a cup of tea – I'd decided to skip breakfast and just eat a cracker. (After all, I didn't want my stomach to bulge in my new outfit!) Then I took the dress down from the cupboard and laid it on my bed. It was stunning and yet simple – showing all Claudia's good taste. It was made from a clever mixture of lycra and silk and it fitted me absolutely perfectly.

I tried not to think of the price when I saw the designer label, but as I pulled it over my head and zipped myself up, I began to feel a million dollars. I shook out my hair and turned to look in the mirror. I have to admit, I even surprised myself. The dress was short and it clung to all the right bits of me, making my legs look very long. My auburn hair looked shiny and sleek against the lime green silk and even my dusting of freckles didn't look too bad!

I made up my eyes lightly – just some brown eye shadow and mascara – and stepped into high-heeled shoes the same colour as the dress. Claudia had given me a cream silk jacket in case the day was cool, and a hat to match. I slipped them on and turned once again to the mirror. Why was I hoping Charlie would think I looked great? I adjusted my hat, told myself not to be silly, stuck my tongue out at my reflection in the mirror, squirted some scent at my neck and headed for the door.

It was Saturday, and some of the lads had finished their early duties and were lounging around having breakfast and watching TV. As I went through the sitting room, there was a low whistling.

"Hey, man, did you see our very own Becks?" I heard. I grinned at them. "Somethin' else!"

"Thanks, guys!" I called over my shoulder.

"Have a great weekend, don't do anything I won't be doing!" Carrying the picture, I ran carefully down the outside stairs almost slap bang into Charlie, who was just coming up them.

"Whoa!" he said, stepping back. And then I saw his face. His blue eyes suddenly had a deeper look in them and I thought I saw a trace of a blush under his golden tan as he took the picture from me and led me over to the waiting truck.

"You look great, Becky," he said after a moment.

"You don't look too bad yourself," I said. Which conveyed nothing of what I *actually* thought. He looked fantastic! He was wearing chinos and a white button-down shirt, and a silk tie with vivid blue flowers, the exact colour of his eyes. His jacket was navy blue and he had on dark brown Kickers. Casual, but stylish and smart. Wow!

"Kelly's loaded Paddy into the horsebox, just like you said, and I think you'll be kind of surprised when you see him," said Charlie, smiling.

I looked into the trailer and could hardly believe my eyes. There was my dear old Paddy, his grey coat shining as much as the mahogany of the tack room, and with a scarlet satin ribbon plaited into his mane and tail. Round his neck was a wider scarlet ribbon, waiting for the picture to be attached.

"Kelly!" I breathed. "I can't believe it! Paddy looks fantastic! I've never *seen* him look so sleek. You must have been working all night."

Kelly grinned sheepishly. "I kinda enjoyed it," she said, "I really love Paddy, and he polished up so well!" she said, laughing.

I gave her a quick hug and turned with Charlie to get into the truck. Lucky the dress was stretchy, I thought, as I hauled myself into the cab. Charlie had obviously cleaned it out thoroughly for the trip, and there wasn't a trace of mud or dust to be seen – nothing that could possibly dirty my clothes.

"Looks like you've groomed the truck as much as Kelly's groomed Paddy," I said, laughing at him.

He nodded. "Can't have you arriving at

Colette's place looking dirty," he said, as he started the engine. Colette was Claudia's sister, and I knew that she had a magnificent house. They were from one of the old-established Maryland families.

We didn't talk much on the drive over to the wedding, and I was busy taking in the countryside. We passed several large houses, with white-pillared porches and drives lined with impressive trees, and surrounded by acres of land. It was almost like something out of *Gone With the Wind*. I was lost in my own reveries, thinking about Grudie and the training programme I was developing, and getting excited at the prospect of seeing Ned and Claudia, when Charlie turned and said, "We're here, Becky. Take a look."

I don't know quite what I'd expected, and I suppose the large houses we'd passed should have given me a clue, but I was still completely amazed at the sight before me.

We'd stopped at some tall entry gates where a man in uniform was standing in the doorway of a small guardhouse. Charlie pressed the entry phone and he came towards us.

"Charlie Mann," he said. The guard looked inside the cab and jerked his thumb at the horse trailer.

"And this guy?" he asked.

"Yeah, this is a horse called Paddy's Pet – he's coming as part of the bride and groom's wedding present – and this young lady is the groom's granddaughter," Charlie added.

The guard looked at the list attached to his clipboard.

"OK," he said, pressing a button inside the lodge door. The gate swung open and the driveway wound its way through an avenue of trees. We drove until we came to an elegant white building with huge porticoes and dark green shutters at the windows. Opulent cars were lined up in the drive and an overflow had begun in the paddock adjoining the garden. There were uniformed men everywhere, parking cars and directing people inside the house.

As we pulled up, one of the guards came towards us. "Mr Charlie!" he said, his black face beaming. "It's a long time since we saw you – too long."

Charlie looked pleased to see him too.

"Hi, Sam," he said. "How are you? And Emmy and the kids? They must be through high school by now."

"They sure are, Mr Charlie," said Sam, nodding. "Bigger'an me now, and all set on their careers. I was real sorry to hear about your father, Mr Charlie. Came as a shock to both of us, I can tell you. Seemed so sudden. And kinda strange, too, he knew that road like the back of his hand . . ." His voice trailed off.

"Let's talk sometime, Sam," said Charlie. "Say hello to Sam Junior and Patrice for me. And I guess Emmy's helping inside, right?"

"Sure is, Mr Charlie. She'll be so happy to see you. Miss Claudia told me to direct your car with the young lady right around the house to the rear courtyard – but I wasn't expecting a horse as well," he said, shaking his head and laughing.

"No, she didn't know that, either," Charlie told him. "It's a big surprise, so I'll just drive it round the back, OK?"

"Yes, sir," said Sam. "You take care now, Mr Charlie, and you too, miss," he said, looking in at me and smiling. "Enjoy the wedding."

Charlie drove cautiously round the house and pulled up near some outbuildings. He jumped down from the cab and came round to help me.

"OK, Becky," he said. "Let's get Paddy out and the picture fixed round his neck, and then I'll go through and find out when you should make your entrance."

He walked back to the trailer and opened the door, pulling down the ramp. He unhitched Paddy, talking to him calmly, and led him down the ramp.

Paddy whinnied in greeting when he saw me and I put my hand up to pat his neck.

"No you don't, you brute!" I yelled, as Paddy did his usual trick of trying to stand on my foot and nudge me in the chest with his head. "Not when I'm wearing my smart gear!" I said, laughing and trying to hold him away from me.

Charlie had fetched the painting from the pick-up, and while he held Paddy, I tried to fix the painting on to the red satin ribbon round his neck. This wasn't made any easier by Paddy tossing his head up and down and getting excited.

Eventually, I managed to hook the picture on to the ribbon, just like Kelly and I had devised the day before, and took the leading rein from Charlie.

"I'll be back in a second," he said. "Then you can both make your entrance." And he was gone.

There were catering staff scurrying around to and from the house and the outbuildings, carrying trays of food, buckets of ice and sprays of flowers. I stood watching everything, trying to keep Paddy away from my shoes.

Soon, Charlie returned, looking pleased. "You're on," he said. "Ned and Claudia are coming downstairs in about two minutes, and then you and Paddy can make your entrance, just before the judge gets going with the wedding ceremony."

"OK," I said, my voice trembling a little. I suddenly felt nervous again.

I followed Charlie through a side door which led out on to the gardens at the back.

Nothing could have prepared me for what I saw – huge landscaped gardens, fringed by woods and rolling pastures. To my left were two tear-shaped swimming pools with tables covered in pale pink cloths dotted around them. Over the tables and arching away from us towards a marquee were pergolas with pale pink balloons entwined in them, forming an archway for the guests and the bride and groom.

Over to my right, on a large terrace, was a full dance band (Claudia and Ned loved dancing) with sun glinting on the brass instruments, and ahead, in the marquee, was a string quartet, already playing some Mozart. Through the two broad bands of guests I could see the figures of Ned and Claudia, standing facing each other in front of the judge. Momentarily, I was rooted to the spot, but a whinny from Paddy and a nudge from Charlie made me move forward, threading our way across to the marquee and the red carpet. Paddy and I walked under the arches of pink balloons towards the bridal couple.

A wave of murmuring and gasps of

laughter made Ned and Claudia turn round, and you can imagine their surprise! There we were, Paddy looking so shiny and beautiful, his big head proudly holding the painting which was slung low on his neck on the scarlet ribbon. And me, trying not to wobble on my high heels and sucking in my stomach for all I was worth, leading him up towards them.

As we stood in front of them, I could see to my horror that Ned's eyes had suddenly filled with tears, but he was smiling. He came towards me and kissed my cheek.

"My beautiful Becky," he whispered. "Looking just like your beautiful mother."

For one awful moment, I thought I might cry, too, but Claudia's voice, all gravelly and sexy, cried out "Becky, darling! How wonderful! Everybody! My new granddaughter and my beautiful horse!" And Claudia, looking stunning in a lavender silk dress and matching coat and hat, and with diamonds and pearls gleaming at her throat and ears, turned to her guests and made a sweeping gesture in our direction. Then everyone was smiling and nodding and all the tension of the moment had gone.

The judge cleared his throat, called everyone to order, and Paddy and I, at this moment like a bizarre couple of bridesmaids, stood behind Ned and Claudia while he read out the short and simple wedding lines. When he'd finished, and Ned and Claudia had kissed each other, the quartet struck up and everyone started talking and kissing the bride and groom. That was that! Ned was now well and truly married, with a capital "M".

I was never quite sure just what made Paddy flip. But quite suddenly, after the quartet had been playing for a few minutes, he reared up, taking me by surprise, and I dropped his leading rein. He swung round, the picture dangling precariously from his neck, and trotted, wild-eyed, back down the red carpet, dislodging a froth of pink balloons as he went. He turned left – spying a large expanse of grass, with a fence and freedom beyond – just as the band began playing *In the Mood*. He reared round on his back legs and careered across the entrance of the marquee again – where we were all frozen in horror – and trotted towards the swimming pools and the buffet and the tables with their neat little pink cloths!

I was literally rooted to the spot, where I was standing with a girl of about my own age. She was wearing the tightest, tiniest skirt I'd ever seen, and balancing on high, platform shoes. She grabbed my arm.

"Quick!" she gasped, pulling me down the red carpet, following Paddy's trail of disaster. She towed me back towards the house at full speed, and we both wrenched our hats off and abandoned them on the first table we passed.

"Sam! Sam!" she yelled. And as if out of nowhere, Sam appeared, running towards us.

"Yes, Miss Pammy?" he said, looking surprised.

"The horse has escaped and he's headed for the pool! He's gone crazy! Can you get Henry out here to help catch him?"

I have never seen anyone move so fast, and Sam wasn't young! But he dashed into the back regions, calling for Henry, and the next thing we knew they were both running past us again, heading towards the pool.

Outside, I was dimly aware that Charlie and Ned were moving across the gardens towards Paddy. They were talking to him calmly from a distance, as he stood, nervous and excited, a bunch of watercress hanging from his mouth, next to the far end of the buffet table. The stunned and frightened guests and serving staff were clutching each other in terror, not knowing in the least what to do and Paddy, a mad look in his eyes, was stamping on the corner of a pale pink tablecloth which was draped gracefully over the buffet.

"Isn't this just the most exciting thing?" breathed Pammy in my ear, her face alight with amusement.

"Oh, Paddy," I choked, extracting myself from Pammy's grasp, and stumbling over to him on my high-heeled shoes. Just as I thought! Paddy had a real sense of fun, and seeing me and with Sam, Henry, Charlie and Ned, all closing in on him, he decided he wanted a bit more excitement. He veered round again, and trotted happily towards the rose gardens beside the marquee. As he weaved his way between the bushes, some of the pink balloons festooned around his head and neck, began to pop. Surprised, Paddy plunged off across the rose beds, leaving a trail of trampled blooms and crushed bushes in his wake. He even stopped to chomp one, just to see what it tasted like!

But now, Sam and Henry had reached him and were standing either side of him, holding out sugar lumps. Charlie and Ned were walking towards him, calling out soothing words as Henry inched his way forward, holding out his hand with the sugar lump in it, and saying, "Come here, boy. Come to Henry now."

As the circle of people closed in on him, Paddy looked as though he didn't know which way to run. He tossed his head up and down, as if he was about to make a run for it, when Henry stepped forward and grabbed the leading rein, still holding out his other hand with the sugar lump in it.

Paddy reared up again, the pink balloons making him look like a bizarre creature on a carousel, as they hung in clumps around his ears. But he spotted the sugar lump (always his favourite thing) and sensing he was cornered, he decided to be a good boy and eat the sugar instead.

I came up behind Ned. "Ned, Claudia!" I gasped, turning to try and find her. "I am *so* sorry! I don't know how I managed to drop the rein – I think the orchestra must have given Paddy a shock!" Tears were pricking at the back of my eyes.

"Darling!" said Ned, wrapping me in his arms. "No great harm done! It's certainly made it a day we'll never forget!" And he kissed my cheek, just as Claudia came up behind me, putting her long arms round me, too.

"Darling Becky! Wasn't that just the funniest thing? What a wicked horse that is, my own darling Paddy! Now you're not to worry, you hear? See, Sam and Henry have everything under control and my guests have never had so much entertainment in their lives!"

And that was how I first met Pammy. She linked her arm through mine and steered me towards the bar.

"What you need is some champagne," she said, grinning. "I've had so much fun and now you must tell me all about yourself. I'm dying to hear. My Aunt Claudia has told me lots about you , but I want to hear it all from you."

As we stood at the bar, gratefully sipping our champagne, I had a chance to get a good look at her. Her hat abandoned, I could see short blonde hair, which was gelled up into spiky peaks, and ears with at least three rows of gold and diamonds in them. Her tiny black dress was like a tube and revealed her gawky figure. She was taller than me, even without the high shoes, but there was something in her greeny-brown eyes that I liked immediately. There was a lively, mischievous look in them and a bright intelligence that I responded to.

"Wasn't that something!" she breathed, in a voice rather like Marilyn Monroe's. "Now come on, let me hear *everything* about you."

"We-ll," I stammered self-consciously, not knowing where to start. Why do I always feel so English and inhibited at times like this? But I began to blurt out all about Ned and our lovely house in England – and Sue and Ben Mainwaring, and the stables, and Paddy and Red Rag, and how Claudia had persuaded me to come over and train Grudie, and Bret King and everything – all in a rush, gulping my champagne between sentences.

"And who's the man in your life?" she asked me bluntly.

I stammered stupidly, looking at my feet. "Um, well, there isn't one really, just a jockey I know, called Jamie. But he's really busy and successful and I'm over here, so well, you know, we're just keeping in touch, but it's nothing heavy."

She looked at me, unbelieving. "Really?" she said. "Now, don't you think that Charlie's rather cute?" she asked, leaning towards me and looking over at Charlie disappearing round the corner of the house with Paddy.

"Well . . . " I stammered again. "I hardly know him yet and—"

"I haven't seen him in ages," she said, "and now you're over at Bret's place, I'll be able to visit with you and get to know him a little better. Last I saw of him was when we were in high school, and I've got some catching up to do!"

So that was Pammy! She turned out to be a friend from the start. As if sensing the sudden wave of unhappiness I felt at the sight of Ned and Claudia disappearing off on their honeymoon, she turned to me and said:

"You know something, Becky? You need some more of that champagne while we get to know each other better!"

CHAPTER SIX

Sunday was spent recovering from the wedding and finding out about Grudie's training programme. I put in some time at the computer, devising some changes and looking at his diet. I wanted to put him on a feed that wouldn't get him over-excited but would build up his stamina, so he was going to be eating less protein and more carbohydrates. I had some ideas about his exercise programme, too, but I was going to get my first solo ride on Grudie over with before I fixed it with Max.

The next morning, as I mounted Grudie in the yard, the air had a definite smell of spring about it. Grudie had a spring in his step to match the season as we trotted out towards the gallops, both of us tense with anticipation. As I led him into a gallop, his ears began to twitch in their usual funny way, and I could feel his lip beginning to flap up and down in excitement. I took him on one whole circuit before we even attempted a jump and then I felt ready. Grudie had steadied slightly but I could feel the energy through his strong back legs and sensed he wanted to take the next fence.

We galloped up the slight slope towards it, my heart thumping at the thought of the big fixed rails and Grudie was pulling like crazy, eager to get at the jump. I had a difficult job to hold him steady and keep his strides even, he was pulling so hard. And then, quite suddenly, we were soaring up and over the top – Grudie's head held high, his legs curled up underneath him and we were down, landing safely on the soft ground.

I slowed him before the next jump, knowing that he would pull away from me because of his impetuous nature, and trying to keep him steady. But it was difficult. He was raring to go and I was finding it very hard to hold him back to a stride that would take us over safely. The wind whistled past my cheeks as we approached the fence at an amazing speed and I could feel his stride wasn't right. We were placed all wrong as we came up to the jump, hurtling through the air and arching up and over the timbers. We were too fast. He hit the top rail, twisted, and fell on landing. I rolled up into a ball and then gradually turned myself over to see what had happened to Grudie. He had stopped not far away, puffing and looking excited, but no harm done. And at least he wasn't galloping back to the yard. I would have felt a real idiot if he'd arrived back before me! What would Max have thought of me then?

I stood up, brushing down my jodhpurs and calling to Grudie. Amazingly, I caught him without a problem and, talking to him soothingly, I ran my hands over his legs. As far as I could tell, he was fine. I hoisted myself into the saddle and trotted gently back to the jump. I wanted Grudie to take a good look at the size of it in a calmer way, so that he wouldn't forget the next time! Then I knew I had to go and face Max. It wouldn't be easy – confessing that I'd allowed Grudie to fall, but I had to do it.

Max and Charlie were standing waiting for us in the centre of the yard, the lads milling around in the background. I could see Bret and Rick in the golf buggy, drawing up to the office – and I have to admit, my heart sank!

Charlie caught hold of Grudie's reins and I dismounted. I couldn't help noticing how great Charlie looked this morning, his blond hair brushed back, revealing his tanned face and vivid blue eyes and his figure in jeans and a blue cord shirt looked lean and fit. But I also felt calmer when I saw him – he had the same effect on me as he had on the horses!

"Mornin', Becky," said Max. "How'd you get along with Grudie today?"

"Good morning, Max," I said, bracing myself for a full confession. "I put Grudie at a couple of practice fences, but he's so eager that we came a cropper at the second one. I just couldn't hold him in check. He's so strong! His head was too high approaching the fence. He wouldn't listen and he hit the top rail – he stumbled on landing. No damage done, thank goodness."

In my usual way, I'd blurted out everything in one fell swoop. Why did I always do that?

"I have a confession to make, Becky," said Max. "I was taking a look through my binoculars from up on the stairs there," he said, pointing at the lads' quarters. "I just had a feeling that's what was goin' to happen. Now, what's your plan?" he asked me.

I gulped a bit. "Well," I said, and I knew I just had to get this right, "I've been thinking all weekend about a series of exercises for Grudie – to help him be more controlled and athletic. It's something I've done with a couple of horses in England, and the results have been fantastic. They're really horse gymnastics," I said, hoping I sounded convincing.

At least Max didn't look *too* sceptical.

"Sounds interestin'," he said, nodding. "It's sure new to me. How about you, Charlie?" he said, turning to his Assistant Trainer.

"I read something on it just the other day," Charlie told him, "but it hasn't been tried on horses in the States yet."

I smiled at Charlie gratefully.

"OK," said Max. "Scott, you take Grudie

and go and walk him around to cool off. Then settle him back down in the stable," he called. "Right, Becky, how about you, me and Charlie going over to the office and figurin' out a routine for our boy? I wanna get this worked out on the programme before I go off to the horse sales in Baltimore tomorrow. Let's go!" he said. Max was full of energy and enthusiasm, and I was relieved that he trusted me enough not to condemn my ideas straight off.

The three of us headed over to the office. Bret and Rick were walking out as we approached.

"Ah, Becky!" Bret boomed at me. "And Max. I want to hear all about what this young lady's planning for my wonder horse, and the sooner the better," he said, towering over me. I was beginning to get the feeling that this race meant life or death to him!

Rick was skulking behind his father as we passed by and made our way into the office.

"Good morning, Becky," he breathed at me as I nodded at him. "Hear you took a tumble on that horse of ours. Lucky no harm came to him – I dread to think what Dad would've done if it had, he's got a lot riding on that horse, if you'll forgive the pun." And he smiled in a sickly kind of way.

"Thanks, Rick," I said under my breath, then turned to the others. "Right, Mr King, Max, Charlie, can I just take you through my exercise and feeding plan for Grudie?"

I just hoped I looked more confident than I felt as I launched into my ideas for Grudie's regime and outlined the new exercises. I suggested that we should start by introducing some interval training, instead of long gallops, to let Grudie settle. I explained that the interval training would be short, sharp work, with one- or two-minute walks in between. For instance, six furlongs, steady canter – walk two minutes – six furlongs, strong canter – walk two minutes – six furlongs, gallop. I suggested to Max that we should also start to lead him off another horse, like Jupiter, for example, who was quiet, so that Grudie would be more settled on his hacking days. Having a rider seemed to make him more anxious, and this way he would have no rider.

These exercises would all be aimed at developing his agility and through that, more control, so that he'd know exactly how to use his strength and courage when it came to the race. I suggested we should use coloured show-jumping fences, set up in a grid, to teach Grudie to shorten and lengthen his stride and be quicker with his feet, which would help him when it came to racing.

When we'd both finished talking, I realised that Max and Bret had been quite silent and I was beginning to wonder what they thought. Then Bret heaved himself out of his chair, and his huge bulk seemed to fill the office.

"Right," he said, "that's it! Get on with the work-out today – there's no time to waste if Grudie's entered in the two lead-up races before the Hunt Cup. And Charlie, you're in charge when Max goes off tomorrow. I don't want anything – repeat anything – to go wrong, you hear? If it does, I'll hold you personally responsible. That clear?"

"Sure, Bret," said Charlie, "I understand. Everything's going to be fine, just fine."

"I sure hope so, Charlie," said Bret. "I sure

hope so." And with that, he turned and left the office, calling Rick to follow him.

The atmosphere lightened immediately they'd left, and we all seemed to let out a sigh of relief. Max went into his office to study some brochures on the horse sales.

"Coffee, Becky?" asked Charlie, as Max shut his door. I nodded gratefully. I felt I could have swallowed at least four cups after that little lot!

Charlie poured me some coffee and we sat at the small table near the computer, chatting about Grudie. The warm sunshine was flooding the office and making Charlie's hair shine like crazy. I was beginning to fancy him, I have to admit, and the wonderful spring weather must have had something to do with it!

"That Rick is something else," I said to Charlie, sipping my coffee. "He looks sly and he comes on too strong."

"Yeah, I know," said Charlie, "but to be fair to Rick, you should know a bit more about him."

Then Charlie told me that a couple of years

before, he'd been driving Rick on his motorbike when they'd had an accident. They'd both come off, but Rick had had his leg trapped under the bike and some serious damage had been done to his ankle. That explained why he walked with a limp, something that would be with him for the rest of his life.

"He thinks it was all my fault," said Charlie, looking into his coffee mug, "and I can't say I blame him. It was just one of those terrible accidents. But Rick wanted to run the stables and he was a real good jockey, too. Now I'm Assistant Trainer and he can't ride as a jockey any more, and he feels his life is pretty miserable. On top of that, his mother left home when he was little and Bret uses him like a doormat. I think he loves Rick, but he sure never shows it – and Rick is always in his shadow. The poor little rich kid. It's hard for him."

Well, I wasn't so sure. But at least I knew something about why Rick was *quite* such a slimeball and certainly the accident made me feel sorry for him. No wonder there was such tension between the two boys, you could feel it in the atmosphere.

Charlie broke the silence. "There's also something else," he said. "It's not just the accident that's causing the problems between Rick and me, and Bret. I haven't wanted to talk about it before, but I think you should know."

Then Charlie explained that, before he died, his father Dick had invested all his money with a firm of brokers which had gone under and he'd been forced to sell his horses to Bret. Bret and Dick were already business partners, and Bret had needed Dick for his connections, especially because of his real estate deals, and Dick's background and knowledge. Apparently, he'd been a brilliant business consultant and, with his Harvard education, knew all the right people.

From what Charlie told me, Dick had been a caring and intelligent father and clearly Charlie had been devastated when he'd died in the car crash.

"Do you mind if I ask you how it happened?" I asked him, tentatively.

"No, that's OK, Becky, I think I know you

well enough now," he said. I felt myself glowing with pleasure. "Apparently, his car just spun off the road on a bend, for no reason that anyone could work out. It crashed through some scrub and dropped down into a ravine." And here his voice cracked. "It exploded on impact so my father would have died instantly. What I don't understand," he said, almost to himself, "is how it happened. Dad was such a careful driver and he knew the road like the back of his hand . . . " his voice trailed off.

I felt guilty that I'd asked him about the accident now, so I put out my hand and laid it on his arm. "I'm so sorry," I mumbled inadequately.

Charlie looked up and seemed to shake himself free of the memory. "That's OK, Becky," he smiled. "Look, you must come out to our place soon. I've got a mare in foal that Dad kept after he'd sold all his other horses to Bret. She's beautiful and I'd just love to show her to you."

"I'd like that, Charlie," I said, looking into his eyes.

"Right now," Charlie said, breaking the sombre mood, "let's get going on the computer, and you can programme Grudie's new exercise work-out into it. Then we can go over his diet together. OK?"

"OK," I said, smiling at him.

I'd learnt a lot in the last hour and now at least I knew why there seemed to be a feeling of friction between the two families. I was really getting to like Charlie a lot, (and not just because of his great body, either). And I knew that he and Max, and even Bret, had been impressed with my plans for Grudie. For the first time I really felt that I was glad to be there.

CHAPTER SEVEN

Jamie
A quick note to let you know I'm feeling much better! I've worked out a new exercise programme for Grudie – The Wonder Horse. Like the ones we used on Rocket for the Grand National, remember?

The wedding was brilliant, but Paddy decided he'd have some fun, too, and nearly wrecked the whole event! Luckily, things were rescued with the help of Pammy, Claudia's niece. She's great and she's coming over to visit today! She's so wacky and funny and I'm really glad I've met her.

Max and Charlie are being very kind and seem to like my plans. We're entering Paddy, ridden by Charlie, for one of the lead-up races to the Hunt Cup. Can you imagine our dear old Paddy racing with some of the top horses in America? I hope it doesn't go to his head! Speaking of bigheads... there's something really weird about Bret and his son Rick, but I can't put my finger on it.

Hugs and kisses,
Becky

That morning, Charlie and I rode out to the gallops together – Charlie on Paddy and me on Grudie. We'd decided to enter both of them in the lead-up races, and I was thrilled that Charlie had said he wanted to ride Paddy. He didn't ride as a race jockey so much now that he was Assistant Trainer to Bret, but he seemed to be taken with the idea of riding Paddy.

As we rode the course, looking at the practice fences, I could tell that Grudie was just as eager as ever, and was suffering no after-effects from his fall.

We decided that Charlie should take Paddy over first, and Grudie and I would ride second. My heart was in my mouth as I watched Paddy jump over two timber fences. He'd never tried anything quite like them before and I felt quite tense with excitement for him. But Charlie had wonderful hands, and he sat still and calm as he and Paddy sailed over them. As they cantered back towards me I could see a look of pure happiness and elation on Charlie's face that transformed him. I began to realise how sad he'd been looking before, obviously still upset about Dick's mysterious accident.

"You were great, Charlie!" I called as they approached. "Well done, Paddy! I don't think anyone would recognise you back home!"

"He's a good ride, Becky," Charlie panted, as he reined in alongside me. "He's got heart, this horse of yours, and strength, too, and with the right training, he'll make a good race, I'm sure of it."

Charlie and I had a fun morning, putting the horses through their paces and schooling them over the jumps. We discussed Grudie's new exercises again and I could see that they were beginning to make real sense to Charlie as we studied Grudie's capabilities – his strengths and weaknesses – on the gallops.

We arrived back at the stables, warm and glowing, pleased with our morning's work and engrossed in discussions about routines and diet as we walked the horses through the yard.

"Well, well, and don't you two look cute!"

I looked up to see Pammy, wearing a black bomber jacket with her tight black jeans worn over shiny black high-heeled boots, leaning on a red sports car as shiny as her footwear! She was smoking a long cigarette and wearing dark glasses.

"Pammy!" I smiled. "Great to see you."

"Hi, Pammy," said Charlie. "'Fraid you'll have to kill the cigarette. Stable rules," he grinned.

"OK," said Pammy, grinding it out under her heel. "Now don't get stuffy with me, Charlie, you know it's ages since we've seen each other and I want to get to know Becky. Show her a good time while she's over here."

She looked knowingly at me.

"Sounds fun, Pammy," I said. "But I'm not sure I'm going to have much time before the big race. I'm going to be really busy with Grudie."

"I think we'll let you have *some* time off," said Charlie, smiling at me. "Even though it won't be much, I'm afraid, with the two lead-up races and everything."

"You have to eat lunch, don't you?" asked Pammy. "Let's go grab a sandwich and catch up," she said, taking my arm.

"That sounds great," I told her, handing Grudie over to Scott. "Let's go up to the lads' kitchen and we'll make something. Coming, Charlie?" I asked him, looking over my shoulder as Pammy pulled me towards the staircase.

"Later," he said. "I'm just going to check on the lads and say goodbye to Max. We've got a couple things to get sorted before he goes this afternoon. Catch you later." He raised his hand, and walked towards Max's office.

"OK, let's go!" said Pammy. Honestly, you'd think I'd known her all my life. We picked our way across the yard towards the staircase.

"Now listen, Becky," said Pammy, still with her arm linked through mine. "I want to take you out to dinner tonight. Why not bring some people along for fun? I guess you need to get to know them a bit better, too."

"Well... " I said, looking doubtful. "Perhaps a couple of them could come. Maybe Kelly and Scott and Karen and Dave, and we could ask Charlie if he was free."

"Oh yes," giggled Pammy. "Charlie's so cute, too, you must ask him. Now, where can we get some food around here?"

I led her up the staircase, and we stopped to look over at Bret's place, just as I'd done on my first night there.

"Wow!" breathed Pammy. "I knew Bret had a big spread, but I guess I didn't know it would be quite that amazing!"

We turned and walked into the sitting room where the kitchen was. We made some lunch and decided to take it through to my room and eat it on the little balcony in the warm sunshine.

"Now, let's plan our evening's entertainment," she said. "I just adore having fun!"

Charlie couldn't make it because he wanted to stay late at the yard in Max's absence and go over some schedules for the horses racing in other spring meetings, so Pammy and I and the lads set off about five-thirty to a town not far away. We thought we'd go to a drive-in movie-cum-burger spot and then on to a place where kids hung out.

I'd never been to a drive-in before, and I really felt as though I was in a movie myself that night – a bit like *Grease*. Pammy kept me giggling throughout the entire film, needless to say, while we munched on our burgers and later, drove into town. Pammy had decided that we'd go to a local bar where there was live music and dancing.

The bar itself was massive with a dance floor at one end – a huge open space with tables and chairs round the edges – and the bar at the other. A band was playing and, as we walked in, Pammy waved at a couple of the guys who were singing.

"Hey, Pammy!" they called between songs. She really seemed to know loads of people, but I suppose it was a pretty small community. At least three guys came up to her, as we made our way to get a cola, and some of them were pretty hunky, too.

"OK, it's on me, kids," she called to them.

The guys gathered around us and Pammy introduced me.

"Hello," I said, casually.

"Oh, *hello*!" they said, mimicking my English voice. I could tell it was all in good fun, even though it was boring, but as the evening wore on, and more beers went down their throats, the teasing got a bit heavy.

The guys in the band started up again, and this time, it was a two-step.

"We often do country dancing here," Pammy shouted in my ear to be heard above the music. "It's real fun, once you get the hang of it!"

"Well, now, little English horse-trainer, Becky," one of the guys drawled. "I just bet you can't do this dance, right? I guess you'd like me to show you how."

"Go on, Becky!" the lads encouraged me. "You can do it!"

To save face, if nothing else, in front of my new friends and work mates, I turned to the guy who'd challenged me. "I bet you ten dollars I can do it perfectly!"

"OK, that's my girl! But I'll still bet you twenty dollars that you can't!"

I found myself being nudged and pushed on to the floor by Pammy and being grabbed by the arm by Scott. Suddenly, I was being twirled and flung about to the infectious music. I wasn't worried about the twenty dollars – it was as good as mine already! One evening, at home, Claudia had taught Ned and Jamie and me to do the two-step. It was after dinner one night when she'd insisted on rolling up the carpet and showing us all herself. Little did I know then just how useful it would be!

I managed the dance brilliantly, though I do say it myself, cheered on by Pammy and the rest of the lads – and by half the bar, as well, judging by the noise! Finally, the music stopped and Scott and I, leaning on each other, breathless and hot, fell into two chairs at the edge of the dance floor.

"Great, Becky! You were just great!" Pammy and the lads crowded round us, patting us on the back and smiling. The guy who'd made the bet sauntered across to me, grinning.

"Well, I guess you deserve the twenty dollars, English Becky," he said. He pulled out the dollar bills and, bowing low, handed them to me.

I laughed. "Drinks on me now, everyone," I panted. I divided up my winnings with all the lads – Pammy wouldn't take a share – and we ended the evening feeling happy and exhausted.

Later that night, having said goodbye to Pammy and promising I'd be in touch with her soon, I said goodnight to Kelly and Scott and the others, and told them I'd check on Grudie and Paddy myself – just so Grudie could get used to me.

I watched them disappear towards the other stables and then I walked across to Paddy and Grudie.

"Hi, Becky?" I nearly jumped out of my skin with shock, particularly when I saw who the voice belonged to. It was Dan Ricardo, that reporter, again. He had a slightly furtive air about him, and had obviously been into the office – there was nowhere else he could have come from.

"Do you always go sneaking around like this?" I asked him, my heart thumping stupidly. "And what were you doing coming away from the office?"

"Look," he said, putting his hand on my arm. "I'm real sorry. I was having a word with Charlie about you earlier on, and I'd been sitting in the office with him chatting about that horse you're training for the Hunt Cup, and, well, we didn't notice the time. You OK?"

"You mean Charlie's still here?" I asked, surprised.

"Well, no, not now," he said. "I was just taking a look at a couple things back there. Research, you know the kinda thing?"

"Sure," I said, sounding quite American, I thought. "But don't make a habit of it, will you? My nerves won't stand it."

"Tell me, Becky, now I'm here, do you know how Bret King finances these racing stables? I know he's big in real estate. Did he entice you over with promises of big money? And what drove you to want to train horses in the first place?"

"Well," I said, thinking it was a strange time of night to be giving an interview. "I'd always had a passion for riding and used to help out in Sue and Ben Mainwaring's stables in my free time. I always knew I was happiest being with horses and after I'd help to train Red Rag, who won the Cheltenham Gold Cup, I was even more convinced—" I came abruptly to a halt as Dan interrupted:

"Is Rick involved in the King empire? Does he handle any business deals himself?"

The nerve! Dan wasn't the slightest bit interested in *my* story – he wasn't even taking notes – and he seemed more curious about Bret's business deals than in the things I was telling him about my life! He was looking over my shoulder at the lamp-lit Barn and the office!

"Look, don't bother to ask me questions if

you don't want the answers," I told him grumpily.

"Oh gee, sorry, Becky. I'm right with you. And thanks for that. I'd better hit the road now, it's getting late and you must be pretty tired out."

And he turned and walked away from me, his stone-coloured chinos looking ghostly in the dimly-lit yard.

I shook my head. He was weird. Bret had obviously given him the OK to explore the stables and talk to everyone, but I'd be very interested to see exactly what kind of article he was going to come up with when he wrote about me when he hadn't even bothered to listen.

That night, after such a great time, I slept wonderfully. I was really happy that I'd gone out with the lads. It was all down to Pammy, to be honest. She'd persuaded me to go, and now I felt I knew them all, especially Pammy, much better! But I couldn't help feeling puzzled by my encounter with that journalist.

CHAPTER EIGHT

One evening later that week, Charlie and I were loading the new training programmes into the computer. We were laughing about something that had happened that day. Paddy had rolled in his stable, and managed to get all his rugs twisted round to the front. It looked for all the world as if he was wearing a huge baby's bib! As we laughed, our eyes sort of locked together for a moment, and time seemed to stand still.

"I guess I'd better get back to this," said Charlie finally. He'd been frozen to his seat for what seemed ages, his fingers over the keys. He typed in something and then stopped, looking puzzled.

"That's weird," he said to me, his face

glowing in the light from the computer screen. "How did I get into that? It looks like a load of details about real estate deals – dates, places, names, that sort of stuff. I can't make it out."

I was peering at the screen over his shoulder but before I could see much I heard a familiar sneer.

"Well, *well*, what's going on here?" It was Rick. Just the person we wanted to see. "A cosy little tête-à-tête round the computer, I see!"

"Rick!" said Charlie, turning in surprise. "Maybe you can help? What's this stuff on the screen that I've gotten in to? Has Bret been putting data on to this computer instead of his own? You know about his business, don't you?"

Rick looked shifty. "Sure I do," he said defensively. "But I'm not at liberty to explain it to you guys. It's all top secret – know what I mean?"

It crossed my mind that he hadn't a clue, probably just wanted to cover up the fact that his father never told him anything.

"Take a look," said Charlie, making room

for him. But Rick had something else to say.

"Dad asked me to come over to check everything's running smoothly. If anything goes wrong with Max away, you'll be in serious trouble. I should exit that file right away as it's obviously none of your business," he said, looking at Charlie.

Talk about Mr Nice Guy!

Charlie was still looking intently at the screen and hardly noticed Rick's insulting tone. I sat down at the computer next to him to see if I could make out what the information was all about. I took in names and dates – something about a resort project – and began to get engrossed in trying to figure it all out. Charlie got up and started sorting through some print-outs I'd done of Grudie's exercise schedules, and I was aware of Rick, muttering to himself as he moved things about on the bulletin board.

It was then that Dan Ricardo appeared. Again! I thought to myself. He was beginning to crop up everywhere.

"Hey, guys," he said. "More in-putting on the computer for those spoilt horses tonight?"

And he walked over to me, looking over my shoulder at the screen.

"Hi, Dan," said Charlie, turning round from his pile of paper. "No, it's just something we got into by mistake."

I looked at Dan's face and saw that he was completely riveted. He was scanning the information rapidly and intently. What was so interesting here? I wondered.

Then he put his hand lightly on my shoulder, said a brief, "I'll leave you to your busy lives then. Goodnight, all," and was gone.

Charlie turned to Rick. "Any ideas on this info yet?" he asked him, nodding towards the computer screen.

Rick looked angry. "I'll discuss this with Dad myself," he said, hostility showing in his face. "But let me remind you that I know more about business than you'll ever know, Charlie, and *certainly* more than your poor innocent father did!"

I've never seen anyone change so fast. The normally even-tempered and calm Charlie turned rapidly to face Rick.

"How *dare* you?" he said. "How dare you

insult my father! You can say anything you want to me, but leave my father out of it, you hear?"

"So-*rry*!" said Rick, sarcastically. "I guess I shouldn't have mentioned your dear departed dad. Well, goodnight, folks, sleep tight!"

Rick left just in the nick of time! Charlie was rigid with anger, and I could tell he'd only just been able to stop himself punching him. I was really beginning to hate Rick! How could he *be* so vile!

"Oh Charlie," I gasped, tears pricking my eyes. "Rick is just *horrible*!"

"Don't worry, Becky," he said, his voice sounding calmer now. "I wouldn't dirty my hands on him. He's not worth it any more. There was a time when we were close, but now . . . I guess he's the way he is because he really does blame me for that motorbike accident."

As he said this, Charlie was looking quite distracted, as though his mind was somewhere completely different.

"Charlie, are you OK?" I asked him, putting a hand on his arm.

"Oh, sure, Becky," he said. "It's just that

I'm kinda curious. Rick was more than just his usual endearing self when he saw what I'd locked into on the computer – he looked flustered. He tried to bluff his way through it, saying he'd discuss things with Bret. But I have a funny feeling he's up to something."

It seemed to me now that Rick might be trying to get back at Charlie, blaming him for his limp and for ruining his riding career.

It was a rotten end to the day, I thought, as I started to pack up for the night. Charlie exited the file and switched off the computer.

As we left the office together, and Charlie turned to lock the door, I spotted Dan Ricardo in a far corner of one of the stable blocks, caught in the glow of the lamps. He was speaking urgently into his mobile phone. That was odd. Why was he *still* here? Was he up to something, too? And if so, what was it?

I turned to say goodnight to Charlie. He still seemed lost in thought as he spoke to me. "See you in the morning, Becky. Get a good night's rest." And he turned and walked off into the night.

The next morning, early, Bret descended on the stables. Charlie and I were standing in the sunshine, circled by the lads, with Charlie giving them their orders for the day, when we saw the buggy zoom round the corner from the ranch house.

Bret had Rick with him. He was looking furious.

"To the office, please, Charlie. You'd better come along, too, Becky," he said, jerking his head in my direction. "And I mean now!" he roared. The lads looked stunned as Charlie quickly finished his instructions. He walked towards the office, followed by Rick, who was looking particularly shifty this morning.

"I want an explanation!" boomed Bret as we walked in. He seemed to loom even larger in the small office. "Rick tells me you hooked into some business information on this computer last night. That right?"

Rick shifted from foot to foot.

"Sure, Bret," said Charlie, shrugging. "It was kinda strange. A load of business details — nothing I could make out. I was curious because my father's name was listed, but I couldn't get a handle on what it was all about and Rick didn't seem to know either. I guess I just got into a programme by mistake. Was it details of some kind of investment my father was involved in?"

Bret's colour had gone from red to purple, but he didn't have a chance to say anything before Charlie went on.

"I know Dad was advising you on some new real estate deal when he died – was it something to do with that?" I could tell he didn't understand what all the fuss was about.

I thought Bret was about to explode.

"So just what did you understand on that screen?" said Bret through gritted teeth. "You think you recognised some names there?" and he looked across at Rick. His son looked down at the floor, but stayed silent.

"No, nothing – really, Bret – absolutely nothing at all, that's why I'm asking you."

Clearly, Bret had to believe that Charlie was telling him the truth, but he was beginning to seem anxious and confused and not just angry. I turned to Rick, who was looking evasive. Was he trying to hide something from Charlie *and* Bret?

"So you really couldn't make head or tail of it?" said Bret, suspiciously.

Charlie nodded. "I barely looked," he said. "It was an accident that that screen came up at all. "

"Well, it had nothing to do with your father," Bret said. "Just a few out-of-date bits of information, that's all. I haven't used it for some time. But Rick works on this computer, don't you, Rick? Maybe you were using it for a data base. That right? What code did you use to hook into it?"

Bret seemed very curious and I could see Rick shifting from foot to foot again.

"It really was just some kind of accident," repeated Charlie. "I can't even remember what I punched in. I thought I input the code for Big Red – obviously I was wrong, I realise that now."

"Sure, Dad, that was it," said Rick. But he looked nervous. There was something about him that I just couldn't trust.

"Well, OK," said Bret, reluctantly. "But

don't mess around again, just keep to the horses' data, that clear? Now let's move on," Bret said to Charlie. "And remember, I want everything to go real smooth while Max is away. If anything goes wrong in his absence, I shall hold you personally responsible.

"There are some mighty important things resting on Grudie right now. So make sure that his training and feeding programmes are being followed to the letter, understood? And that goes for you, too, Becky. I'm real pleased with what you've done with Grudie up to now – just make sure things stay that way." And snarling at Rick to follow him, he walked out into the yard, into the buggy and swung round the corner to the drive.

"Phew!" I breathed. "I feel as though a hurricane's just been through the place!"

Charlie nodded, shrugging his shoulders and smiling at me.

"Sure, I know, that's Bret for you. I just wonder whether Rick's up to something," he muttered, almost under his breath. "I just wish I could find out. But right now, Becky, we need to concentrate on those warm-up races. Let's get back to work."

Charlie picked up his jacket from the chair and led me out into the sunshine once more.

CHAPTER NINE

As I stretched out in bed the next morning, I was feeling quite luxurious and at the same time excited by the prospect of the warm-up race at the end of the week. Charlie would be riding Paddy and somehow I felt it would bring us closer together. I had to admit, I was really beginning to like Charlie – a lot!

A pang of guilt swept over me as I thought of Jamie. Well, we had come to an agreement about leading our own lives while I was over here – and England, and everyone, did seem very far away. I could see how things were between us when I got back, but meanwhile, I'd just let things happen . . .

I jumped out of bed, had a quick shower and decided that I'd try and look a bit more stylish today. Though whatever Pammy said, it really wasn't possible in a stable yard. I yanked on one of my skinniest tops and put on my favourite shirt loosely over the top – I loved its black and white checks. Then I pulled on my tightest, stretchiest black jodhpurs, bent over, flung my hair back – I was ready. I looked at myself in the big mirror as I was going out of the door. Not bad, Becky. The Maryland air certainly seemed to agree with me, and the clear spring sunshine had already started to give my face the hint of a golden tan. It was too bad about the freckles across my nose, I just hoped Charlie didn't hate them too much.

When I got down to the yard – having grabbed a couple of waffles and a cup of coffee (American coffee was so good!) – I was greeted by a strange scene. A string of horses had just got back from the first lot (in Bret's stables it was at seven o'clock) and Charlie was standing holding Jupiter's reins and talking earnestly to Scott, the lad who'd been riding him on the gallops. Charlie's face was tense.

"What happened, Scott?" he was saying, as the other lads dismounted and gathered round

Charlie.

"I think he may have pulled a tendon," said Scott, his face anxious and pale. "We'd only done two gallops and suddenly he pulled up, lame. I—"

"*What?*" shouted Charlie, his usual calm expression gone. "But you read the programme for today, didn't you? The one I logged into the computer yesterday for Jupiter? I expressly said no galloping whatsoever. You were supposed to do only six-furlongs at half-speed!"

Charlie bent down and tenderly felt Jupiter's leg. The horse flinched and started backing away, pulling his head up.

"That's it," whispered Charlie, running his hands over his hair. "That's just what he's done by the look of it, pulled a tendon. And that's going to be one heck of a long job to heal. Becky, get on the phone, will you, and ask the vet, Doc McClusky, to come right over. The number's in the stable phone book. Tell him what my diagnosis is and that it's urgent, will you?"

As I nodded and ran over to the office, I

saw Rick. He'd obviously arrived just as the horses had returned to the yard and had overheard what had happened. Right now, he was jumping into the buggy – to go straight over and tell Bret, I was sure. What a sneak! Especially now Max was away, he knew exactly how Bret would react.

For a moment, I stopped in my tracks.

"Becky, get on to it, will you?" called Charlie. "I want McClusky here pronto!"

"Sure. Sorry, Charlie," I said, running to the phone. What on earth was Bret going to say when he found out from Rick what had happened? He was bound to blame Charlie. He'd already told him he'd hold him personally responsible for anything that went wrong in Max's absence. Oooh! The little —! words just couldn't express what I was feeling about Rick at that moment.

The next morning, Charlie and I rode out on Paddy and Grudie, to go over the timber practice fences again and to see how the exercises had improved Grudie's control and athleticism.

The vet had confirmed Charlie's diagnosis on Jupiter and told him that it would be another three weeks before he could even be walked again. It would mean that he'd miss his important spring races. Charlie told me that, luckily, Bret was away for a couple of days.

"Rick made a point of letting me know he'd phoned Bret and told him what had happened," said Charlie. "'I was just being helpful', as Rick put it."

He really did seem to have it in for Charlie, one way and another, I thought, as we rode up the gallops. He was obviously so bitter about the accident that he'd stop at nothing to get rid of him.

Charlie and I had a wonderful time that morning. He helped me put Grudie through his paces. The grid work had backed him off his fences, and the interval training had proved the answer to calming him down generally.

At the end of our session, we turned for home, both elated and with all thoughts of Rick's nastiness forgotten. My face was tingling and Charlie's eyes looked even bluer, I noticed, as I shot him a glance from under the brim of my riding hat.

As we entered the yard, we saw Kelly running towards us.

"Charlie!" she gasped, reaching up for Paddy's rein. "Another horse has come down with an injury! Scott told me to come and get you straightaway – I was about to try and raise you on your mobile," she panted.

Charlie dismounted quickly, and handed Paddy over to Kelly. "Which horse is it?" he asked urgently.

"It's Jacko, I'm afraid." Her brown eyes looked troubled.

Charlie walked quickly over to the stables. "Look in on me when you're through, Becky," he called over his shoulder. "If I'm not in Jacko's stable, I'll be in the office. I'm going over to check Jacko's programme – make sure it was followed."

I dismounted, leading Grudie back towards his stable. "What exactly happened?" I asked Kelly.

"Well, Jacko had been out for his daily exercise and was perfectly fine. We cooled him down, walked him around, groomed him – all the usual routine. Then we gave him his first feed for the day. A little later he started to have a muscle spasm in his hind legs. He was in a lot of pain. It was horrible, Becky. I ran out to find you both as soon as Scott told me. What's happening around here, that's what I'd like to know?"

I left Kelly and Dave dealing with Paddy and Grudie, and walked towards the stables. I saw Charlie cross the yard at the far end and stride into the office. I found myself running after him, anxious to find out what had happened.

As I entered the office, Charlie was sitting at the computer, tapping in the code for Jacko's daily programme of exercise and feed. We both waited for the details to flash up, and I could almost hear our hearts thumping with anxiety at what we might find.

"I knew it!" breathed Charlie, turning round from the screen. "I went through all the routines last night and I remember exactly what feeding programme I'd ordered for Jacko for today. And it's all been altered!"

"Charlie, are you sure?" I asked him, looking over his shoulder at the screen.

"Look!" he said. "It's been changed. I didn't specify that he should be given that much protein! I'd never make that mistake, Becky, take my word for it."

I took a look at the instructions that Charlie had input the night before. Too much protein with the amount of exercise that Charlie had prescribed would certainly have caused azatorae! And that would have led to the muscle spasm in Jacko's legs and back. Jacko was prone to azatorae and even the smallest increase in the amount of protein would trigger it off.

"Oh Charlie," I gasped. "This is dreadful. What's happening here? You're always so meticulous with your daily routines. There's no way you'd have made this mistake in the diet. So who's been tampering with the programmes? And why would they want to cause harm to the horses, anyway?"

"I don't know, Becky," he said, sighing, "but I know that when Bret finds out – and I'm sure he will – my head's going to roll.

Listen, right now I must get Doc McClusky over again. I want him to check out Jacko for anything else."

"Right," I said, trying to look more positive than I felt. "I'll see you later and we'll go through all the feed and exercise programmes together, last thing tonight, and make sure nothing happens to them. OK?"

"Right, and thanks, Becky. We're going to have to get to the bottom of this before something else goes wrong!" he added, resolutely.

As I walked towards the lads' kitchen for a cup of coffee, I saw Rick talking to Scott over by Jacko's stable. Could it be him? Did he feel so bitter about Charlie that he'd cause harm to the horses in Max's absence knowing that Charlie would be held responsible? Right then, I knew he was the last person I wanted to talk to, and I pretended I hadn't seen him. Charlie and I would have to make absolutely sure that the office and the computer were completely secure tonight after we'd gone over all the horses' routines for the next day.

Startled out of my preoccupation, I jumped

as Dan Ricardo appeared in front of me.

"Hey, Becky," he smiled. "Deep in thought? I hoped I'd run into you or Charlie. I've just heard that another horse has gone sick – something to do with being given the wrong feed?"

"Look," I said tersely, "it's none of your business! And it certainly wasn't Charlie's fault, he'd never do anything so dumb as order the wrong diet for any horse. He's a brilliant trainer!" I surprised myself at my vehemence.

"Well, OK!" he grinned. "I'm not accusing anybody. Just wanted to know the story, that's all," he said, holding his hands up in mock surrender. "Got any ideas about who might have been playing around with the programming? And why they'd want to?" he asked.

"No, I have not, and I wouldn't tell you if I had!" I spat at him. "Maybe you'd like the story. Well, you seem to have been hanging around the office a lot, and you've had just as much opportunity as anybody else!" As soon as the words were out of my mouth, I wondered if they were true. But that would be crazy! Dan didn't have a motive – did he? It was much more likely to be Rick who wanted to get rid of Charlie.

"Look, Becky," Dan was saying defensively, breaking into my confused thoughts. "I'm just here to get an angle on the stables now you're here. You know, 'British girl brings success to billion dollar Bret King's stables'. You know the kind of thing?"

But something in his face left me feeling anxious. I was sure he wasn't telling me the truth. I brushed past him into the kitchen. One thing was sure though – I really didn't want this guy anywhere near me right now!

CHAPTER TEN

That night, after Charlie and I had gone through the training and feed programmes for the next day and made sure all the office windows and the doors were securely locked after us, we went up to the lads' deserted sitting room for a cup of coffee. We'd discussed changing the password needed to get into the computer files, but Charlie felt that, as all the key Barn personnel needed to know it anyway, it would be a pointless exercise. We couldn't spend all our time wondering who might have tampered with the horses' programmes.

Instead, we sat down in the comfortable sofas, sipping our drinks, and Charlie told me more about the Maryland Hunt Cup and the warm-up races before it.

"The Hunt Cup didn't develop on its own, Becky – it was the first timber race in Maryland, but other races soon followed. My great-great-grandfather, Edward, was one of a group of young men who organised the first Grand National Point-to-Point. I think they thought if the English could have their Grand National, why couldn't we have ours!"

I smiled, imagining how things might have been in those days and loving hearing Charlie talk.

"The next race that was organised was called My Lady's Manor Point-to-Point. It was started by the sporting inhabitants of the Manor. Sometimes the location of the two races changed, but soon a natural progression developed. Both the Manor and the Grand National were run over three miles, unlike the Hunt Cup, which is four. But now the Grand National's become a bit more difficult than the Manor, and less difficult than the Hunt Cup. More coffee, Becky, and stop me if I'm boring you to death!" said Charlie.

But I was happy to be there with Charlie,

relaxed and talkative, and in any case, I really was interested in the history of the big race that I was training Grudie for.

I smiled at him. "Yes, more please, and no, I love hearing about the race!"

"Well," he went on, "it takes a very strong horse to run timber races, against pretty tough competition, and for three weeks in a row. Hunt Cup fences are enormous, about four feet eleven inches, some even up to five foot three. The warm-up race fences are much smaller, but they're all fixed upright timber – not brush, sloping fences like English steeplechasing. They're the kind of fences that need accurate riding and *very* careful jumpers. You can't afford to make any mistakes over these guys. Over sloping fences you can meet on a bad take-off stride and get away with it. But not over fixed timber rails.

"Some competitors decide to skip one of the warm-up races altogether. My grandfather actually owned and rode one of the only two horses ever to have won all three Maryland fixtures on successive Saturdays!

"I think that's why my father was so

passionate about his horses and the Maryland traditions. Grudie winning this race means a lot to me, too, Becky, and it's not for the same reasons as Bret."

Charlie stopped for a moment and looked down at his hands. "I just want you to know, Becky, that I don't resent your being here, taking over Grudie's training. I have to admit, I did feel angry at first when Bret told me about bringing you over. But I knew I'd reached the end of my ideas on his training, and so had Max. We can both see that your exercises have made a world of difference to his performance."

I blushed, pleased that Charlie had realised that I might be feeling awkward. After all, Grudie had been bought on the advice of Charlie's father, and they had both been very involved with the horse. If Grudie won, it would be a testament to Dick. For Bret, it would just mean glory and money.

"I think we should only run Paddy in one of the warm-ups, don't you?" Charlie was asking me now, changing the subject slightly.

"Yes, if you think so, Charlie. This is just

another learning curve for Paddy. As long as he's fit, and I think he'll do well enough, that's all that matters."

There were no more incidents at the yard. The horses' programmes were intact, and we all felt a buzz of anticipation at the thought of the first lead-up race. And now, Saturday was here.

I'd woken up long before my alarm clock went off, but made myself a cup of tea in my room and began to get ready. I would be wearing Claudia's colours for the race (I really missed Ned and Claudia. I'd had an ecstatic postcard, written by Claudia, giving me their address and phone number in Aspen). I knew Ned would be loving the early spring skiing there and was glad that the honeymoon was working out so well for them both. All the right social life for Claudia and fantastic mountains and snow for Ned.

I dressed in my cream racing breeches and a well-cut black jacket, and for the race, I would pile my hair up into the jockey hat I had to wear. I pulled on my best black racing boots, picked up my sports bag and went to have breakfast with the lads.

Kelly and Scott were in the kitchen and I could feel that we were all rather nervous. None of us could eat much, but I was sure we'd make up for it afterwards. Pammy was bringing a huge hamper with picnic lunch and drinks for everyone, which was really nice of her. Even though she did admit that it would be Emmy who'd be doing it all for her!

Charlie was outside in the yard waiting where, a short distance away, the vast horse trailer had drawn up, ready for its occupants. The goose-neck trailer was attached to the pick-up truck, and they were all painted in King livery colours.

Karen and Dave were leading Paddy and Grudie towards us, and both horses had obviously had the grooming of a lifetime! Their coats shone and their breath plumed out in the chilly morning air. The sunshine hadn't yet burned off the mist that clung to the tree tops everywhere. I shivered.

"Nervous?" asked Charlie, standing next to me.

"You could say that," I grinned, nodding.

"You'll be fine just as soon as we get going," he promised. "I'm looking forward to showing you some of our beautiful Maryland countryside."

He was right, but as we approached the race site, I began to feel nervous again. Charlie, sensing it, kept up a calm flow of conversation, telling me where we would be parking the horse trailer, where the tents with the check-in tables were and how big the crowds would be.

As we stationed our horse trailer on the site, I looked around. It was bigger than our point-to-point venues, but not as large as our Grand National. It had a friendly feel to it, I could tell already.

From then on, we all became involved in our own particular jobs. First, Charlie and I went to register our names and then we walked the course. The fences were much the same as the practice fences at home, but Charlie pointed out various places that were difficult. The downhill run to the last fence had always been a feature of this race, he told me, but it had caused too much trouble at the bottom of the run. In the end, the finishing line had been moved further forwards, but it still needed accurate timing. The rider had to take care not to go too fast downhill and get the pace all wrong for the last fence, especially difficult when the horses were sensing the end of the race.

When we'd put on our racing clothes, Charlie and I made our way to the weighing-in room. Here it was all so familiar to me that I started to calm down. Charlie and I, side-by-side but not talking, walked to the saddling-up enclosure. It seemed only minutes till we were riding towards the starting line, and then, miraculously, we were off.

I felt I had to pinch myself to make sure I was really here – in the States, racing in one of the best known warm-up races for the Hunt Cup. Except that I couldn't, of course! I was far too busy concentrating and talking gently to Paddy as we galloped over the three-mile course. The fixed timber posts were three high in some places and four in others – and they were big! But Paddy remained calm and took everything in his stride. We managed to ease past three horses, and I kept Paddy steady, pacing him for each fence as it came up.

About halfway round the course, I saw Charlie and Grudie pull right away from the rest of the field, with only two other horses up with him. It looked as though they were going well! I was more pleased with that than I was with dear old Paddy, but I pulled my concentration together quickly before I let the race get away from us altogether.

The rest of the race went brilliantly for Paddy and me, and we managed to come in fifth. Grudie and Charlie were second! I was thrilled. As we cantered slowly back to the unsaddling enclosure, where the trainers, owners, lads and riders were gathering, I could see Charlie was elated. Grudie seemed perky and fit, only puffing slightly, and almost looked as though he could run another race.

"He was great, Becky!" called Charlie, panting more than his horse. "Just fantastic! He's so much more controlled."

We both dismounted in unison, smiling and grinning at each other stupidly. "You're a real genius, Becky," Charlie cried, and he took my arm and pulled me close to him, kissing me full on the lips.

"OK, OK, break it up!" It was Pammy, of course! "Just because the horse ran well, there's no need to get all yukky about it!"

"Hi, Pammy!" we said together, turning to greet her. And I could tell she was very nearly as pleased as we were that Grudie had done so well.

"You look incredible, as always," said Charlie, smiling at her.

"Thanks, Charlie, you look cute yourself," she added, giving me an enormous wink. "Those riding breeches sure make the most of a man."

I think Charlie began to blush, because he turned and started giving instructions to Scott about cooling Grudie down.

"Lunch!" said Pammy. "And then I'm going to tell you about the little celebration shopping trip I have planned." And she hooked her arm through mine and steered me in the direction of her beautiful car.

Pammy did look incredible! She was wearing clothes that weren't entirely suitable for the races, but they certainly made her stand out from the crowd. She had tight zebra-print trousers, high black patent leather ankle boots, and a white PVC bomber jacket. Her hair, as ever, was sticking up in platinum blonde spikes, gelled in place to prevent them collapsing in the slight breeze that was blowing away the chilly mist.

The warm sun was appearing fast, and I felt wonderfully relaxed, as you do when you've used your muscles and done something well. Pammy and I opened both the rear doors of her sports car and stretched out luxuriously on the back seat, the large picnic hamper between us.

"Hey, Charlie!" she called over to him, waving her dark glasses. "Bring the guys over, will you? We've got a ton of food here. And I want you to open the champagne. This is just the first of many to celebrate," she said, turning to me. "And now, here's what we're going to do later this afternoon. We're going on a shopping trip and we're going to spend some serious money," she said, confidingly. "It's going to be real fun!"

Later, much later, I lay flat on my bed, my arms and legs stretched out full-length. I was wrecked. There had been no telling Pammy that I was too tired to go shopping after the Manor race and the champagne. She'd had her heart set on it, so that's what we did.

We'd abandoned the lads and Charlie and the horses – all with Charlie's approval – and driven off in Pammy's car to the nearest big town. We'd walked the length of "the only street worth looking at in town" as Pammy described it, and eventually, after going in and out of every designer shop there was, we found some clothes that Pammy thought I just *had* to have.

First, we'd bought a tight black ribbed top which clung to the curve of everything curvy on my body, and to go with it, some long, long leopard print trousers. I didn't know if this was really me, but I found it useless to put up any resistance.

Next, she made me try on every dress in the boutique she'd selected for our second purchase. The staff were very patient, but I was getting more and more weary, plodding out time after time to show her yet another little dress.

Finally, she screamed in delight, clapped her hands and said, "That's it, sweetie! That's absolutely it! Eat your heart out, Cindy Crawford!"

Relieved, I turned and started walking back to the satin-lined changing room. On my way, I glimpsed myself in the ornate tilted mirror. For a moment, just for a moment, I thought I had come face-to-face with Cindy Crawford – but then I realised it was me. The assistant had moved my hair around, so that it looked stylish – as though I'd just got out of bed, but much better. That, combined with the lipstick that Pammy had made me try at a beauty counter, and the dress, had really changed me. The dress was very simple, really. It had tiny bootlace satin straps and was cut low across the top of my breasts. It had a black satin underslip, with a chocolate-coloured lace over the top, and it stretched and moved with my body. It was very short and Pammy had made me try on a pair of high-heeled shoes that exactly matched the black satin. It was sensational!

I must have looked completely stupid as I stood there, dumbstruck, gazing at myself. But Pammy's voice broke my trance.

"Get changed, Becky," she was calling in her husky voice. "We're going to a very special place for dinner." And I felt as though I'd only just eaten lunch!

So here I was – exhausted and happy after one of the best days of my entire life. Pammy had arranged to meet Charlie in one of the chicest spots in town, and all three of us felt on a high as we ate oysters, followed by lobster and then the most delicious mango sorbet in the world. It had all been wonderful. Charlie drove us all back to the Barn in Pammy's car, dropping me off first (Charlie at least could see I was whacked) and then Pammy was going to drive Charlie home on her way back to Colette's house.

Did Charlie fancy Pammy? I wondered, as I lay on my bed, too exhausted to get up and undress. Well, I didn't care. It had been a brilliant day – Grudie had gone like a dream, Paddy had done well, and Charlie had kissed me! Nothing could go wrong now!

CHAPTER ELEVEN

It was a couple of days later, when Charlie and I were doing the rounds after lunch, that he noticed something wrong with Grudie's leg. It looked swollen and tender.

"Take a look, Becky," said Charlie, running his strong, gentle hands down Grudie's leg. "I'm pretty darn sure he's got a heat in it."

I bent down to feel the leg and Grudie tensed as I touched the slightly swollen, hot patch, just above the joint.

"Oh, Charlie," I whispered. "You're absolutely right. This couldn't have happened at a worse time, with only one warm-up race safely behind us."

"I know," he said quietly. He seemed calm but I noticed that muscle in his jaw again and his face was tense. "Look," he went on, "the only thing I can do is wrap a poultice round it which should draw out the swelling and the heat. It'll take careful bandaging, but that's something I was taught by my father."

A figure cast a shadow across the open half of the stable door. "Got another problem?" It was Rick, smirking and peering in the doorway.

"Nothing that we can't handle with some careful bandaging, Rick. Grudie has a slight heat in his leg – it happens sometimes. Remember how Dad taught me to wrap something like this?"

To his credit and my amazement, Charlie was chatting to Rick as though he was his brother (and I remembered that once they'd been very close), forgetting the sneering comments he'd been making lately.

"Sure, Charlie. Let's hope you get lucky and it does work, or Dad will be mad as a polecat. He's got a lot on his mind at the moment – there's a serious deal he's about to complete, around the time of the Hunt Cup, and he doesn't want any screw-ups."

"I thought he looked a little more worried than usual," said Charlie, half to me and half to Rick. "Must be something mighty important to be preying on his mind this way. Bret's usually real cool about his business affairs."

"You just do your job and forget Dad's deals, OK? Make sure Grudie doesn't get lame for the next race, or there'll be trouble! And you, Becky, Grudie's your responsibility, too, remember? That's why Dad hired you, so you'd better get it right! Dad's back tonight, so make sure you get this horse fit pretty damn quick!"

Honestly! Rick got worse and worse. I knew he fancied me from the way he stared at me all the time, but he was so rude! Just because he was the boss's son, he thought he could get away with anything.

"Take no notice, Becky," said Charlie when he'd gone. "He's not that bad. He's just always trying to look big in Bret's eyes, always trying to get Bret to praise him. But it never works, I'm afraid. I guess he never really got over his mother leaving, though she wasn't much to write home about, either."

"I can't help it, and I know it's not nice of me, but I just hate Rick. He can't wait to get his own back on you and he takes every chance he can to make you suffer."

Charlie grinned at me, standing up now he'd finished examining Grudie's other legs. "Take it easy, Becky. Come on, let's go and prepare Grudie's bandages and I'll explain the poultice to you. And you take it easy, too, you hear?" he said to Grudie, patting his neck. Grudie waggled his expressive ears backwards and forwards. He was such a gutsy horse, he probably thought Charlie was going to take him out for a gallop, in spite of his sore leg!

The next day, all hell broke loose. As I emerged from my breakfast at about seven-thirty in the morning, I heard a huge commotion coming from the centre of the yard. Bret was standing in the middle of the lads, shouting at Charlie. I ran down quickly to see what was happening.

"You idiot!" he was yelling. "How could you be so careless, and with all that high-and-mighty knowledge from your precious father, too!"

Bret looked round as he saw me coming. "And you!" he shouted. "Grudie's your responsibility, too! Why do you think I brought you all the way over from England and pay you all this money? Because Claudia and Colette told me you were the best, and now look what's happened!"

Charlie tried to intervene.

"And don't try and make excuses!" he roared at him. "You're fired! Pack up your stuff and get the hell out of here, you understand?"

"But Bret!" Charlie looked desperate. "Don't you see, I *know* someone tampered with those bandages. I know *exactly* how I—"

"Don't even think about telling me!" thundered Bret. "I don't want to hear any more excuses. The horse's leg is blistered under the wraps, and you're to blame! Rick!" he called, over his shoulder at his son, who was standing smirking in the background. "I'm putting you in charge. You all got that?" he said, looking round at the entire Barn staff. They nodded, dumbstruck, unable to say anything. But I could tell by the looks on their faces that they didn't like what was happening one bit! And neither did I! No Charlie, and Rick in charge! Life would be awful! Now I was sure that Rick was behind everything that had happened, and all the rest of the things that had gone wrong, too.

"Get back to your duties," said Bret. "And Rick, follow me. We have to work out your role here. Charlie, get packed and make sure you fill Rick in on everything that's happening, you hear?" Bret and Rick walked towards the office and I heard Max's door shut behind them.

"Charlie, what *happened*?" I asked him desperately. "Did Grudie's leg blister?"

"Yes, Becky," he said grimly. "When I went to check on it first thing this morning, I unwound the bandages and the leg was all blistered up – it's a horrible sight. The poor horse is in quite a bit of pain. And as luck would have it, Rick was right with me when I unwound the wraps. He must have gone straight off and given Bret the glad tidings."

"But, Charlie," I said, gulping, "you were trying to explain something to Bret about the bandaging, and the way your father had taught you to do it. What was all that about?"

"Well, I just know that someone tampered with the wraps," said Charlie, stopping and turning to face me. "Dick taught me a special way of doing the bandages, but this one had been done clumsily so it was easy for me to see that it had been bandaged up again in a different way. Someone had put more poultice on, too hot, and that's what caused the blistering."

"Tell him again! Make him listen to you!" I said, my voice beginning to tremble. "You can't leave, Charlie, I'll never be able to cope without you!"

"Take it easy, Becky, you know that's just not true. Right now, I feel angry at Bret, and confused, I can't think straight. I need to get out of here. Listen, Becky, you'll manage just fine, you know you will. We'll talk later. Grudie won't race in the next lead-up, but you'll be great riding Paddy, and I've got faith in Grudie to come up with the big one on Hunt Cup day. It's not a problem."

Charlie turned away, emotion welling up

inside him, I could see. I suddenly felt ashamed. Here was Charlie, fired from the job he loved, and all he'd done was try and make me feel better! In spite of his reassuring words, just how was I going to cope without him around?

The rest of the day was miserable. As if reflecting the mood of the Barn, the weather was dull and overcast, with a fine drizzle that felt more like Irish weather than what I'd come to expect from Maryland. I hated seeing Charlie giving final instructions to the lads and picking up his belongings from the tack room and the office.

I needed a big hug from Ned, and of course he wasn't around. I suddenly felt very lonely at the thought of Charlie not being there, and with Rick in charge while Max was still away, life would be grim. I knew the lads felt the same way, because the atmosphere in the Barn was very subdued. They trusted and liked Charlie, but they certainly didn't feel the same way about Rick.

That night, I felt more miserable than I'd felt for a very long time.

CHAPTER TWELVE

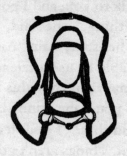

I was woken up the next morning by a frantic banging on my bedroom door.

"Becky! Becky! Time to get up! Here's your coffee!"

It was Pammy! I don't know when I'd been more pleased to see someone.

"Pammy, what on earth are you doing here at such an early hour?" I asked her, amazed that she was even up and about, let alone all made-up and ready to go.

"Well," she started, dropping down on to the edge of my bed while I drank my coffee, "I heard what happened here yesterday, and I thought you might need little old Pammy for some moral support."

"How did you hear?" I asked her curiously.

"I telephoned the office yesterday afternoon to talk to you, and I got Charlie. He told me everything," she said, running her hands through her spiky hair. "And he told me you might be able to use a friend today, so I decided I'd come right over this morning and keep an eye on you," she grinned.

"Charlie said that?" I said, feeling pleased. "Well, he's right. Things aren't going to be the same without him around, especially now Rick's in charge with Max away. Did he tell you what's been happening to the horses, too?"

"No," said Pammy. "I guess he couldn't go into too much detail over the phone. Go ahead, fill me in," she said, snuggling down on my bed, dying to hear the gossip.

So I did. And most importantly, I told her how Bret blamed everything on Charlie.

"But I'm sure Rick's behind it," I said in a low voice, "he just has to be!"

"Well, the story goes that he's never gotten over the accident, that he still thinks his limp's been caused by Charlie's bad driving," she said, conspiratorially. "Maybe he's been tampering with the programmes on the computer, just so's he can get rid of Charlie and have Bret put him in charge instead!" she said triumphantly. "He always had his heart set on being a champion jockey, but when he couldn't do that, and when Bret didn't want him involved in his real estate business, maybe he felt the only role left for him was to be in charge of the Barn. Yes, I'm sure that must be it! Becky, you have to do something. You have to find out the truth and confront Rick with it – tell Bret, so that Charlie can come back. You have to! You have to get rid of that little slimeball!"

"It won't be easy, Pammy, he's pretty devious and I'm sure Bret wouldn't believe me, anyway. Oh, it's all so horrible, and I'm supposed to be riding Paddy in the next warm-up race, and I really don't feel up to it. I know this one's going to be more difficult than the first, and without Charlie here to encourage me, I'm not sure I really want to do it."

"Of course you do!" said Pammy fiercely. "You show 'em, Becky," she said, her eyes sparkling. "Do it for Charlie's sake. I know you can! I'm going to tail you all day, make you cheer up, and if I meet that creep Rick, I'm going to make him wish he'd never been born!" she said, grinning wickedly at me.

True to her word, Pammy followed me on my duties all day. She watched me and Scott examining Grudie and checking on his leg. It certainly looked better today, and I could tell that this time Charlie's bandaging had not been messed around with. She came out in the buggy to watch me take Paddy over the practice fences and we had a hilarious lunch together. In typical Pammy style, she'd brought a picnic – I guessed that the devoted Sam and Emmy had put it together for her – and we ate it outside in the sunshine, watching the few horses out in the paddock.

"You know something, Becky?" she said. "Life is *much* more fun now you're here. I've even been thinking about doing something with my life, too. I know Mom thinks I'm a no-hoper. But my grades at high school were good. I might go to college to do journalism – I was always good at writing. But not until I've had a lot of fun this summer!"

"Talking of journalism," I said. "Did you notice Dan Ricardo hanging around again this morning?"

"Sure," said Pammy. "He was talking to me when you were getting Paddy cooled down after your ride. He was kind of curious about where Charlie was. He'd missed the big rumpus, and all. But he wanted to know about Bret's business deals, too. I told him a bit about what I know – that Colette and my stepfather are investors in his real estate business, like most of the prominent folks around here, but I don't know any details."

"Hey, maybe Dan could help you with your journalism?" I said, teasing her.

"Well, he *is* kind of cute, but he's too preoccupied at the moment, he barely noticed me at all, even though I'm wearing one of my best little numbers," she said, looking down at herself.

"Little number" was one way of describing it! Pammy was wearing a lime green vest dress that clung to every curve and some shoes to match. Over that, she had her short black leather jacket and her fingernails were painted to match the dress.

"Just right for mucking out the stables!" I said, giving her a shove. We were sitting on the picket fence, munching our smoked salmon and dill sauce sandwiches (no simple bread and cheese for Pammy).

She turned her huge greeny-brown eyes on me. "*What* did you say?" she squealed. "Puh-*lease*!"

"Just kidding, Pammy," I grinned.

"Well, you little—" and she shoved me back. We both clutched on to each other, giggling hysterically, beginning to lose our balance, salmon and dill sauce hanging out of our mouths.

We wobbled about, clinging on to each other for dear life, until finally we fell, thud, on to the grass below. We rolled about laughing stupidly, unable to stop, holding our stomachs and choking on our lunch. Eventually, exhausted from giggling, Pammy turned over to face me, her lime green dress hitched up and covered in grass, and food all over her face.

"You are the best fun!" she sighed, her eyes glinting.

"Oh Pammy," I said. "You don't know how much better I feel. You've really cheered me up. Thanks for coming."

"Sure, kid," she laughed, "any time." And we hugged each other. "Just make sure you do well in that race, you hear?"

Later, after Pammy had gone, I decided to visit Paddy. The sun was beginning to go down, and there was a pink glow in the sky. Everything looked very beautiful, and I just wished my mood could match it.

Paddy whinnied in recognition in his usual way, and I let myself into his stable, running my hands down his neck and burying my face in his warm, familiar smell. I felt sad and confused again now Pammy had gone. Still, she was right, I *had* to ride Paddy and I really wanted to do well. I felt a sudden wave of determination, thinking of all the people I cared about back home and how they'd always encouraged me.

I said goodnight to Paddy and let myself out of his stable, turning to check the office before I went up and had dinner. As I did so, I saw Dan again, leaving the office and speaking into his phone. Why was he still here? Maybe he'd been chatting to Rick, but Rick was always back at the ranch by five o'clock and it was nearly six now.

I felt a sudden prickle of unexplained fear. He surely wasn't hanging around for more information on the horses or me, or even life in the Barn – he must have got all the background information he needed already. I walked quickly across to the office. The lights were still on but not the computer – everything looked the same. I turned off the lights, and locked the door. There was no sign of Dan – he seemed to have disappeared again.

Quite suddenly, I knew what I wanted to do. I wanted to go and talk to Charlie. I ran up to my room, taking the stairs two at a time, calling "Hi" to the lads in the sitting room on the way. I wrenched off my jodhpurs and dirty shirt, pulled on a t-shirt and jeans and my new cowboy boots, and brushed my hair. I was ready to go.

"Karen," I said, as I walked through the sitting room again, "I'm going over to see

Charlie if anyone wants me. His number's in the book right by the phone."

"OK, Becky," she said. "See you later."

I walked through the long line of stables, checking the horses automatically as I went, to the garages at the other end. The car Bret had allocated for my use, and any of the lads who needed it, was in the second barn.

I reversed out of the garage, turned into the drive and slowed down at the guard's hut by the closed gate. (Bret was security crazy, like most of the rich people around here).

"Evening, miss," he said. "Taking a drive?"

"I'm going over to see Mr Charlie," I told him. "I won't be too long."

"Well, take care, miss," he said, peering in at me, "there's a crazy guy out there. He's been forcing women off the road in their cars and robbing them at knife point. Didn't you see it on TV last night?"

"N-no," I stammered. "I haven't had much time for watching TV."

"Well, you take care now. Have a nice evening!"

At first, I was busy concentrating on

driving the car on the right-hand side of the road. I knew I had to carry straight on until I reached a fork, then turn left (Pammy had given me directions – she knew where Charlie lived because she'd dropped him home after our night out). The sky was darkening and I started to relax. I turned on the radio, which was tuned to the local station. I listened with half an ear.

"Now here's some advice for all those women drivers out there." I sat up sharply at this. *"Don't take any chances. There's a nut drivin' around in the Manor Farm area who's been targetting lone female drivers and forcing them off the road – making them hand over all their money and jewellery at knife point. He's driving an old Ford. So watch out, you ladies. Now folks, here's some cool music to take you through the night. I'm signing off now, so remember– take care out there."*

I switched the radio off and suddenly felt very jumpy. I was alone, in a strange car, in unfamiliar countryside – and somewhere in the area there was a nutter driving around! I gripped the steering wheel more tightly, peering through the dark beyond the headlights for the fork up ahead.

It felt as though I'd been driving a long time, and still no turning, when I noticed the lights of a car behind me in the rear-view mirror. I began to feel nervous, but I told myself not to be silly. Why shouldn't it be a perfectly innocent car? Forcing myself to look straight ahead, I saw the fork coming up. With some relief, I turned left, ready to start looking for the crossroads which should soon appear, and where Pammy had told me to turn right. The car behind me took the left-hand fork, too. Now I really *was* worried!

That doesn't mean a thing, I told myself. There were bound to be other cars going this way. But this one seemed to be gaining, bumping over the holes in the road, its lights dipping up and down as if making an effort to catch up with me. I stepped on the accelerator. Oh please, I prayed silently, please let the crossroads come up soon!

After what seemed like miles and miles, I saw the dimly-lit crossroads looming ahead. I slowed down at the last minute, not wanting the car behind to catch up, and took a quick glance left and right. It was lucky these roads were straight and open, even if they were narrow, I thought, as I swung the car round to the right.

I let out a sigh of relief, feeling now that I wasn't far from Charlie's place. Another mile or so, Pammy had said, and I should see a sign on the left of the road saying Dick Mann – Stud Ranch and Racing Stables. Charlie just hadn't had the heart to take it down, and Dick had never wanted to. From there, it was half a mile to the ranch. Pammy said I would see a curving drive with a white post-and-rails fence and a pretty clapboard house.

The pale-coloured car was still behind me! It had lost ground at the crossroads, but now it was there again! I could feel panic washing over me in waves. I told myself to calm down – but I couldn't. I took deep breaths and tried all the things you're supposed to do to relax. Ned! Claudia! My brain whirled around trying to think what they would be saying to me right now. I'm sure Ned would say, "Steady, Becky. You're OK."

Easier said than done. But there it was! At last, the little white board with a black arrow saying Dick Mann – Stud Ranch and Racing Stables. I was here at last. Driving recklessly now, in a blind panic, I swung off the road into a narrow lane, practically putting the car into a ditch, but swerving just in time to avoid it. Another wild thought came into my mind. What if Charlie wasn't at home? What would I do?

The lights were there again, closing up behind me in the lane and blinding me in the driving mirror.

"Please, please, the drive, where is it?" I moaned out loud, feeling frantic. Then, through the dusk, I saw the glint of a white picket fence coming up on my right. I was there! Just a few more yards and I'd be OK!

I veered across the narrow lane, my tyres screaming, and hit the gravel at speed, sending stones flying up around me. I saw the house appear up ahead, but only the porch light was on! Would Charlie be there? There was no doubt now that the car behind was definitely following me! I saw its lights swing round, illuminating the drive.

"Charlie! Charlie! Where are you?" I gasped. I skidded to a halt in front of the house, the gravel arching up into the darkening sky, lit by my headlights. I turned off the engine and almost fell out of the car, leaving the door wide open, and running towards the house.

"Becky! Becky!" shouted a voice. It was Charlie! He was running towards me across the paddock in front of the house, calling my name (my noisy arrival must have been heard miles away!). I turned round and started stumbling wildly, calling his name.

"Charlie! Oh my God, Charlie! Help! Please – help me!"

I ran full tilt into his outstretched arms, practically knocking him over, shaking and gasping for breath. I turned, in panic, towards the car pulling up behind mine, pointing, unable to speak.

Its door was flung open and a man got out. I turned and buried my head in Charlie's shoulder, unable to look.

CHAPTER THIRTEEN

"Look, Becky, take a look!" said Charlie, trying to turn me round to make me see who had been following me. Reluctantly, I twisted my head, still gasping for breath and trembling.

"See, it's the journalist, Dan Ricardo. Has he been following you?"

"I don't know," I breathed. "I thought he was. Why has he been hanging around the Barn for so long, anyway?"

Dan was jogging across the grass towards us, the light from my headlights throwing him into sharp relief.

"Hey, Becky, Charlie! Listen, I can explain," he was saying as he ran.

Charlie and I stood still, waiting for him to reach us. I'd removed myself from Charlie's shoulder and was standing next to him, pushing my hair back and trying to stop myself from shaking. I'll kill Dan, I thought.

"Becky," he said, stopping a yard or so in front of us, "listen, I sure hope I didn't scare you—"

"*Scare* me!" I croaked, "you terrified me out of my wits! Why are you following me? Just what are you playing at? Haven't you heard about the maniac with the knife?"

"Calm down, Becky," Charlie said hastily. "Let Dan explain. Come on, let's go into the house, it's getting chilly and you need a drink, You're shaking like a leaf."

Charlie put his arm round my shoulders and steered me towards the house. "Come on, Dan, I think you'd better tell us what this is all about."

We went into a wide, square hall, with a round polished wooden table in the centre, and a large blue and white china vase filled with spring flowers. I could sense immediately the atmosphere of a real home, somewhere that had had laughter and love in it. I felt myself begin to relax.

Charlie called out, walking towards a door at the back of the house. "Sarah, we've got company. Can you bring us a jug of hot coffee, please, and some cookies?"

A small, round motherly-looking lady appeared in the doorway of a kitchen, her hair done in a bun and wearing a striped apron over a blue spotted dress. She could have been about sixty or seventy years old, it was hard to tell, as her lively face shone with kindness and her blue eyes looked merry.

"Good evening," she said. "I'm sorry, Mr Charlie, I didn't hear anyone arriving."

"Let's hold dinner, Sarah, please. But coffee would be wonderful. Sarah's been part of the family ever since Mom died of cancer when I was just two years old," said Charlie, turning to me. "She took care of me when my father was away on business and she's still doing it," he added, smiling.

He led us through a door on the left of the hall and we went into a large, low room, filled with more bowls of flowers. There were rugs on the polished floors and several comfortable sofas arranged round the fireplace. At the end,

French windows showed a glimpse of a floodlit terrace and a lawn beyond. Unlike Bret's place, this house showed taste.

"Take a seat by the fire," Charlie said to me. "Dan, you'd better sit here, on the sofa next to me. Now, let's hear what you've got to say."

Sarah had lit the fire already and I sank into the welcoming chair, beginning to feel more like my old self but looking expectantly and still angrily at Dan.

"Becky, I'm so sorry I scared you. I overheard you telling the lads that you were driving over to see Charlie, and I wanted to come and talk to you both here. But I didn't know where Charlie lived, so yes, I was following you. It was only when you started to speed up that I realised you didn't know it was me, and that you were scared. I'm real sorry."

I have to admit, Dan really looked as though he meant what he said.

"Didn't you hear the warning on the radio – the one about the guy who's been following lone women drivers, and then forcing them off the road and robbing them at knife point?" I asked him. "I was terrified."

"No, no way!" said Dan, looking even more guilty. "No wonder you were frightened. Can I explain?"

"I think you'd better," Charlie said, getting up to take a tray from Sarah, who'd appeared in the doorway. "Thank you, Sarah. This should make everyone feel better."

He put the tray on a small oak table in front of the fire, and started to pour the coffee. "Becky, do you think a tot of brandy would help?" he asked me.

"Better not," I said, shaking my head. "I've got to drive home, remember?"

"OK," he smiled. "But get this down you, and have one of Sarah's delicious cookies. I was brought up on them."

I took a mug of steaming coffee, dunked the large chocolate chip cookie into it and took a mouthful. Heaven! I felt better already.

"Go ahead, Dan," said Charlie. "It's all yours."

"Well," he began, "you both know I'm doing a feature on Bret's stables for *Pacemaker*, as well as on Becky, right?" We nodded. "I want to get an exclusive – you know – 'English girl trains billionaire's horse for Hunt Cup'. If I manage to get an exclusive, I get serious money," he said, looking slightly embarrassed.

"Go on," said Charlie.

"Well, when things started to go wrong with the horses, that story seemed even better and I knew nobody else had been allowed into the Barn. I wanted to get an angle on it, find out what was behind it. That's why I came over, to talk to you both – find out the truth behind the accidents."

"I see," said Charlie doubtfully. "So you risk terrifying Becky just so you can get a big fat fee, that right?"

"Look, I've explained, I really didn't want to frighten her, just wanted to come and talk to you both, believe me."

I liked Dan, in spite of him terrifying me half to death, and suddenly I wanted to tell someone else about Rick, and how I felt he'd been behind the accidents at the Barn.

I started to explain all the things that had gone wrong with the horses, and how Charlie and I both felt that the computer programmes had been tampered with. I told him I was convinced that it was Rick who was trying to sabotage Charlie's career, out of spite.

"Sure." Dan nodded. "You may be right. From what I've seen of him, I wouldn't want to have a whole lot to do with him myself. Now, Charlie," he said, changing the subject slightly. "Can you tell me something about your father? I know he was Bret King's partner and business adviser, and wasn't he the one who taught you all you know – ran this place as one of the leading stud ranches in the country? I heard he just died in an automobile accident, right?"

I looked over in sympathy at Charlie, who was sitting very still, his elbows resting on his knees.

"Charlie," I began, "you don't have to talk if you don't want to."

"It's OK, Becky. I really think I'd like to talk to you both. I need to talk to someone about Dad, and it might as well be now."

Then Charlie started to tell us about his family, how it was an old established Maryland family, and they had developed the stud ranch over the past hundred years. Dick Mann had been educated at Harvard, and had contacts with prominent politicians and business people from his Ivy League days. He knew the senator for Maryland, for example, and it was at one of his parties that he'd been introduced to Bret.

"Bret soon realised that someone like my father, with his experience in the racing world and his friendship with politicians and the business community, would be a valuable friend and partner. He persuaded Dad to go into the real estate business with him. For a while, this worked well, even though Bret and my father were very different kinds of people." Charlie stopped and looked at his hands resting on his knees. He had to steel himself to carry on talking.

"Well, when my father lost most of his money in a broking firm that went bust, he was forced to sell all the horses. I guess his one thought then was to take care of my future. So he suggested to Bret that I work for him, at the Barn. I can't say I was happy about it, but I knew I was turning into a pretty good trainer, and I was beginning to have a reputation as a good rider too. So, Bret agreed. But lately I'd been thinking that his decision seemed to have forced my father into some complicated business agreement with Bret. I'd been feeling real uneasy about things – and Dad seemed distracted. He didn't want to talk to me when I asked him what was worrying him. He just told me everything was fine.

"And then the accident happened." Charlie cleared his throat. "Dad was driving along a stretch of highway he knew well – no problems with visibility, or anything – when the car skidded on a bend, got out of control, and spun off the road. The car exploded and. . ." Charlie's voice faltered. He looked so desperately sad that I could hardly bear to watch him.

I glanced at Dan. He was sitting on the edge of the sofa, listening intently to every word Charlie was saying.

"So you see," finished Charlie, "Rick has a lot to gain by getting rid of me. He'll be in charge and he'll be the only person Bret will talk to. He's always wanted to be involved in Bret's business, but so far, his father doesn't seem to have had much faith in him. Now my father's dead, Bret needs another partner and I'm sure Rick wants to be that person – I guess his whole life he's been trying to make his father take him seriously."

"You may be right, Charlie," said Dan, getting up suddenly. "And thanks for talking to me." He turned towards the door. "Great coffee, too," he said abruptly. "I have to go now, and Becky, I apologise again for scaring you."

Charlie led Dan out of the room. He seemed to want to leave in rather a hurry now he'd heard what Charlie had to say. I didn't altogether trust him, in spite of his explanations about 'exclusives'. Perhaps it was just female intuition.

"Becky," said Charlie, coming back into the room. "You're welcome to stay the night – you look tired. How about it?"

"Thanks, Charlie, but I don't want to give Rick any more cause for complaint than I have to."

"Well, at least stay and have some dinner, right here, by the fire. It would do you good."

"I'd like that," I said, nodding, "and it would really help if we could go through the details of tomorrow's lead-up race. I'm feeling pretty terrified and I could do with some good advice."

"That's what I thought," said Charlie. "You'll be fine, and you don't have an early start tomorrow – the course is only five miles away. So let's have dinner and I'll talk you through it, OK?"

"OK," I said, happy at the prospect of this time alone with Charlie, and I really needed help with the race if Paddy and I were to going to come through it successfully.

CHAPTER FOURTEEN

I didn't feel brilliant when I woke up the next morning. My body was stiff and I still felt tired, even though I'd made it back to the Barn for an early night.

I prepared my kit, in Claudia's colours, and stuffed it into my sports bag. "Come on, Becky," I told myself, determined not to feel negative. "Paddy's really going to show everyone how wonderful he is. And you can't let him down."

I ran downstairs, grabbing a muffin on the way, and into the yard where Kelly and Scott were doing their work on Paddy.

"Kelly, I really don't know how you make Paddy look like that!" I told her truthfully.

"I just love this horse, Becky," she said,

reaching up and patting Paddy's neck. "And I sure hope you do well. Scott's driving and I'll be in the back with Paddy, so everything'll go like clockwork. Don't worry about a thing."

I felt better instantly. I'd been feeling so low about Grudie not being able to race, especially after all the good training I'd put in. But the lads were supportive, even if Rick was unpleasant, and I was really very lucky.

"Thanks, Kelly," I said, giving her a quick hug. "I'll be fine."

We loaded Paddy into the trailer and I swung myself up into the cab beside Scott. "OK, let's go!" I said. "One down and two to go!"

After that I was quiet. I just wanted to prepare myself for the race ahead, which Charlie had warned me would be tougher than the first warm-up – more five-bar fences. I could feel butterflies in my stomach. I mustn't let Paddy down, I thought silently to myself.

The familiar buzz of the race meeting calmed my nerves as we settled Paddy and found the place where we had to register. I walked the course with Scott, trying not to let the size of the fences be too daunting. Once I'd familiarised myself with the layout, I just had to ride it! But I had to admit, I still felt out of sorts. Never mind, no doubt I'd feel better just as soon as Paddy and I had taken the first fence.

I couldn't see Charlie anywhere, and I spent my time with Paddy just before the race. Finally, we cantered down to the start, both of us excited by the atmosphere.

And then we were off! The tape was up and Paddy and I were launching ourselves forward, stretching out towards the first fence. I could feel Paddy was eager as we came up the brow of a slight hill and spotted the first timber frame. His feet thundered over the grass and I held myself still, concentrating on the jump ahead. Paddy tried to pull faster, but I held him steady, and we soared over the fence, Paddy pulling up his front legs like a cat. Why had I doubted him?

We made good ground over the first jump and we were up with the first four horses. I relaxed and started to enjoy myself. We thundered round the next curve and the second fence came into view. For some reason, the sight of it sent a tremor through my body. It looked horrifyingly big, and I just hoped my feelings didn't communicate themselves to Paddy.

I kept him steady as we approached, but he started to lengthen his stride too soon! I could feel myself out of rhythm – we were going to mistime the jump! I did everything I knew to calm myself and keep Paddy's timing right, but as we took the fence at a crazy rate, I knew we were heading for disaster.

Paddy fell, catapulting me out of the saddle and landing all wrong, his hoof smashing down through my ear lobe.

I don't remember much about the fall. I know I rolled instinctively into a ball, in spite of the red-hot pain in my ear. I thought, almost calmly, that Paddy had split my head in half. I felt totally detached as the warm blood surged down my neck and inside my shirt.

The next thing I remember was waking up in hospital. The ambulance drive and stretcher ride were all a blur. For some reason I couldn't understand, my eyes didn't seem to want to focus and everything looked very bright. I shut them again, and felt a surge of pain in my left ear. My head felt bandaged and I began to remember the race, the jump and the fall. Was Paddy all right?

It wasn't his fault that I was feeling off-balance. Had he fallen awkwardly? I wondered.

I tried to open my eyes again, and this time, there was a hazy picture of someone by my bed. For one crazy moment, I thought it was Ned. I shut my eyes, feeling hot tears seeping down through the bandages round my face. Ned! If only he really could have been here!

"Becky, Becky," a voice was saying gently. "It's me, Ned. What have you been up to, old girl?"

It must be Ned! Only Ned ever called me "old girl" in quite that gentle way.

I forced my eyes to open again – and there he was! His dear, kind familiar face peering at me anxiously.

"You look very tanned," I said stupidly.

"Skiing, remember?" said Ned, smiling

now. "Welcome back to the land of the living. You're going to be fine."

"Oh, Ned!" I said, memory flooding back to me. "Is Paddy all right? And you're supposed to be on honeymoon! Why are you here?"

"Calm down, sweetheart," said Ned, putting his warm dry hand on mine. "Paddy's fine, no harm done, just a bit surprised, that's all. He pulled up by the next fence, apparently, and then trotted back to you quite sedately. And Claudia and I had a wonderful honeymoon, and it's about time we came back. She's been spending far too much money." And he winked at me.

"How did you know what had happened?" I asked him. "How long have I been here?"

"Pammy told us, more or less straight away – Colette had our telephone number. She'd gone to the race to watch you, but missed you before the start. She's promised to come and visit as soon as she's allowed to. You've been here a few hours, that's all," he added.

"What's happened to me – exactly, Ned? Please tell me, I'd much rather know," I whispered weakly.

"I'm sure you would. Just like me," he said, smiling. "Well, it's been a bit of a nasty one, Becky, I'm afraid. But don't worry, the doctors here are very confident that everything's going to be all right. You were lucky, Paddy could have landed on your neck and done much more damage. As it is, old girl, he put his hoof right on your earlobe – severed a bit off. Now, don't be alarmed, the docs have stitched it all back beautifully. It's a miracle what they can do nowadays, and I'm told that this happens to be one of the leading hospitals in the country for this kind of micro-surgery."

I couldn't take it all in. Ned's calm, reassuring voice telling me about my horrendous accident. But he seemed to think I would be OK. And I trusted Ned – he never lied to me, I knew that.

"H-how long?" I stammered. "How long do I have to be in here?"

"As long as it takes," Ned said. "When the docs say you can leave, that's when you can leave. Take one day at a time, that's all they've told me so far."

I shut my eyes again.

"Just try and sleep now, old girl, then you'll feel much better. I'm going to stay here, right beside you, so there's nothing to worry about."

Reassured, I did just that. What would I do without Ned here? Good old Pammy, I thought, just before I drifted into sleep.

Ned had been right. The sleep had been amazingly restorative, and the next time I woke up, I felt much better and I sat up and ate something. When I saw the doctors, they told me they were very pleased with the results of the surgery and I'd been lucky that the ambulance crew had gathered up the missing part of my ear! Yuk! I really didn't want to think about that.

They also said that, after a few months, I'd hardly even notice the scar. I wanted to believe them, but just at that moment, I certainly looked strange. My head was swathed in bandages and my eyes had bruises round them. I looked like some small hurt animal peering out of a nest. Very attractive!

Today was the first day I was allowed any

visitors, other than Ned. As I looked up from my breakfast, the door opened and Claudia appeared. She looked wonderful, and I told her so.

"I know, darling. The Aspen air and sun, and your grandfather, is just what the doctor ordered!" she breathed in her gravelly voice.

"Now, look what I've bought you. You can't lie here in that t-shirt, you need something to make you feel glamorous."

"Fat chance, with my head looking like a football," I sighed.

"Just wait till you get a look at these!" said Claudia, and she produced a long cardboard box tied with pink satin ribbon. As she undid it and lifted the lid, I heard the rustle of tissue paper.

"There!" she cried, triumphantly. "What do you think?"

She was holding up a pair of soft silk pyjamas the colour of aquamarine. "The same colour as your beautiful eyes," she said. "Now, let's get the nurse to give you a hand with your shower, and we'll try them on!"

It was useless arguing with Claudia. She

persuaded the nurse to help me with my shower and afterwards, she laid out the pyjamas on my freshly-made bed and went away to get a cup of coffee.

I sat on the edge of my bed, fingering the luxurious silk. No doubt about it, Claudia usually did have the right ideas. I slipped them on and they slid smoothly over my skin, making me feel better already.

"Well?" asked Claudia, appearing at my door again. "Now let me see you." And she stood in front of me, turning me gently round to get the full picture.

"Fabulous, darling!" she breathed. "I knew that colour was absolutely right the moment I saw it. Now you'll look stunning when that adorable Charlie comes to visit."

I felt myself blushing. "Claudia! He probably doesn't even realise what's happened to me," I said, knowing that this couldn't be true – he'd said he'd be there to watch the race. "Let alone want to come and visit me," I added miserably.

Claudia didn't pause for a second. "Let's just wait and see," she said.

CHAPTER FIFTEEN

The next day, they were all sitting round my bed, with me lying elegantly (I hoped) on top of it, wearing my new pyjamas. That is, Ned, Claudia and Pammy were there – but not Charlie.

Claudia was getting really excited. Apparently, her first husband, who'd been seriously wealthy, had left her some shares in real estate and they were going up and up – through the ceiling, as she put it. Claudia was busy reeling off a list of companies she had shares in, and suddenly I stopped her, mid-flow.

"Claudia, that's really weird. I recognise some of those company names, I'm sure I do. I think they were on the information that

Charlie flashed up accidentally on the office computer. Something about a resort project. Bear, something or other." I stopped thinking. "He hadn't got a clue what the figures and information were all about, but I know his father's name was there, too." My mind went off at a tangent. "How do you know so much about business, anyway, Claudia?" I asked, teasingly.

"Darling," she drawled, "you'll never get a rich husband if you don't understand the business world, take it from me!" But she leant over and gave Ned an adoring smile. They were certainly a wonderful couple, I thought, forgetting about the stuff on the computer. I just hoped I would be so lucky one day.

Pammy broke into my day-dreams. "Hey, guess what, Becky? I thought I'd go check out life at the Barn while you were cooped up in here, just to say hello to Paddy and Grudie while you're away. Well, Rick sure is being Mr High-and-Mighty around the place – he's behaving like a real jerk. The lads are having a bad time with him, and you know something else?" We all looked at her. "He's looking more and more suspicious, if you ask me."

Pammy was her usual stunning self this morning. She was wearing a puce jumpsuit, zipped up the front – or rather unzipped down most of the front, and revealing a lacy black bra top. She had on baseball boots, which somehow made her less imposing, but I bet the colour of her all-in-one had scared the horses!

Ned and Claudia were looking confused, so I started to explain what had happened to Jupiter, Jacko and Grudie, and how I was beginning to think that Rick was behind the accidents. I told them I was sure he'd interfered with their training programmes on the computer, just so Bret would get rid of Charlie and he could be in charge.

"And now the company names you've been talking about seem familiar, maybe Rick is up to some dirty business deals, as well."

"Rick was never one of my favourites," said Claudia, "but who can blame him with a father like Bret? And his mother wasn't much better. She may have been Miss Maryland 1972, but she sure didn't have many brain cells to go with the beauty. She walked out on Bret when Rick was only five – met some oil man or other. Bret just treated her like a possession, by all accounts, wouldn't let her out of the house or anything. And Rick was always a shy little thing. Now he's shy and sly – not a nice mixture."

I refused to feel sorry for Rick, even though his life didn't sound much fun. I was *sure* he had it in for Charlie.

To change the subject, I turned to Pammy. "How's Grudie's leg?" I asked her. "Have the blisters healed up?"

"I asked Karen and Dave," she told me, "I knew you'd be dying to know about that crazy horse," she said. "They said to tell you his leg is just fine, and they've been going through your exercise programme with him every day. He's coming through well and the leg's not showing any sign of injury. There, OK now?"

I nodded. "And Paddy?" I asked. For some stupid reason, just saying his name made me feel tearful. It made me remember the fall in grim detail. Ned, who never missed a thing where I was concerned, reached over and patted my hand.

"He's fine, sweetheart, truly. Isn't he, Pammy?"

"He's better than fine!" she said. "He's being spoilt to death by Kelly, and she's spending all her free time with him, just talking to him and making sure he's doing OK. You guys and your horses," she sighed, "it beats me what you see in them."

I grinned at her. "Aren't you getting to like them, too, Pammy, just a little bit?"

Pammy made a face. "Give me a cowboy any time, you can keep the horses!" And we all laughed.

Later that day, I was lying on my bed feeling sleepy after lunch, and thinking about what Claudia had been telling me about her shares going up so fast. My mind seemed to be filled with different bits of information as I lay there with my eyes shut, unable to do anything. I heard the door open, and assumed it was the nurse, coming to take away my tray, and I felt so drowsy I didn't even have the energy to open my eyes.

Someone walked over to my bedside and

put a warm strong hand on my arm. Charlie! I knew it was him before I even opened my eyes! I recognised the smell of his aftershave.

"Hi, Becky," he said, bending down to look at me. I don't think I'd ever seen his blue eyes this close before. "Sorry to wake you. How're you feeling?"

"Charlie," I whispered, and stupidly I felt like crying again. Claudia had told me it was the shock of the accident, combined with the anaesthetic, that made me feel so tearful all the time, and maybe she was right. But I felt such an idiot!

I sniffed loudly. "I'm just so pleased to see you," I said, apologetically, trying to pull myself up against the pillows. "I know I look a wreck, my head still swathed in bandages, and my bruises are a horrible yellow colour and—"

Charlie reached out, put his finger on my lips then bent down and kissed me, very gently. Life felt good again!

"I'm sorry I couldn't get here before, Becky," he said. "First of all the doctors wouldn't let you have any visitors, other than Ned and Claudia, and then my mare had her foal. This is the first chance I've had to come visit you."

"Charlie, that's great news!" I knew just how much his one remaining mare meant to him. Dick had kept her when he'd had to sell all the others and told Charlie that she would be the key to building up a new stud ranch. "What did she have? What does it look like?" I asked him now.

"It's a colt. And he's all black, just like his father was. He's just great and as soon as you're out of here, I'll take you over to see them both. Sarah's just as excited as me, she knows my father would be so happy if he were here now."

I squeezed Charlie's hand, unable to say anything.

"Now," said Charlie. "What's the news on your injury? What do the doctors say? I've been telephoning Ned, but I haven't spoken to him today."

"You have?" Ned hadn't told me. "Well, they say it's healing up brilliantly and I can go home tomorrow. That is, to Colette's place for a couple of days, and then back to the Barn. So things are going fine. But Charlie, I'm more worried about you," I ended lamely.

"Me? I'm OK," he said. "I'm keeping busy at home, there's plenty to do, I can tell you."

"No, I mean about Rick. I'm just worried that he's going to do something else to get at you. Look, Charlie, I've been thinking. I want you to ride Paddy in the Hunt Cup for me. Will you do that? I know Bret will find another jockey for Grudie, he won't let you ride him now."

"Yes, I'd really like that," said Charlie, looking pleased. "And you're right, I don't stand a chance of riding Grudie now. I just hope Bret finds someone who understands him."

"But I'm still worried," I went on. "Rick will be furious if I don't give him the ride on Paddy. I know he doesn't do any professional riding now, because of his injury, and he's too heavy, but Pammy told me he expects me to allow him to take the ride, now that Bret's fired you. And she says he's still behaving suspiciously. Who knows what he might do next? Charlie, I'm worried that Rick will do something to harm you – he'd stop at nothing to wreck your career, I know it!"

CHAPTER SIXTEEN

A few days later, and feeling a bit battered but much more my old self, I was sitting in Charlie's big, warm kitchen with Ned and Claudia.

Charlie had invited us all for dinner, but Ned, being Ned, had insisted on doing the cooking. Truthfully, I think he was having withdrawal symptoms. He loved cooking and he hadn't had a chance on his extended honeymoon, and no one except Emmy went near the kitchen at Colette's. So he was looking like a pleased and excited schoolboy as we sat round the scrubbed old table while he stirred and tasted things on the stove.

We were all discussing Rick again, and the accidents with the horses, and speculating on how, and why, they might have happened, when we heard a car draw up outside.

Sarah, who'd been persuaded by Ned to give up her domain – Ned could charm the birds off the trees – answered the door.

"It's that same gentleman who was here the other night, when Miss Becky arrived the first time," she said to Charlie, putting her head round the kitchen door.

"Have him come on through, please, Sarah," said Charlie, getting up out of his wooden carver chair. "What can Dan Ricardo want this time?" he said, addressing all of us.

Sarah showed Dan into the kitchen. He was looking even more dishevelled than usual, his tie pulled down and his collar open.

"Hi, folks. Look, I'm real sorry to interrupt your dinner, but there's something I have to talk to you about."

"Sure, Dan," said Charlie. "Here, take a seat. Would you like a drink? We're having wine."

"No, thanks," he said, flopping down into a chair next to me. "But coffee would be great. I have to keep my mind clear."

"Dan, this is my grandfather from England, Ned Hunter-Davies, and his wife, Claudia," I said.

Ned shook hands with Dan and Claudia smiled at him.

"I hear you took a fall, Becky," said Dan. "Hope you're feeling better now."

"Much!" I said. "Now, what is it you want to tell us?"

Dan took a deep breath and a swig of strong coffee. "I'm afraid I've had to lie to you and Becky, Charlie. I don't work for *Pacemaker* at all, I work for a national newspaper, the *Herald Tribune*, and I've been sent down here to investigate Bret. My editor has been following the Bret King real estate empire for some time, and he thinks Bret's sailing pretty close to the wind. For some time now it hasn't been clear just how Bret is actually making his money, and we're pretty sure he's been involved in things that are against the law."

"What!" I couldn't help myself. I must have had my jaw hanging open in surprise.

"Go on, Dan," said Charlie quietly. He

didn't look nearly as stunned as I was, I noticed.

"I decided I needed your help," he said, looking at us both. "Have you ever wondered whether Bret was behind what's been happening to the horses?"

"*Bret*?" I gasped. "No, we've been thinking it's Rick."

"Well, when those three horses went down with injuries, I was pretty sure that Bret had been tampering with the computer programmes. I know he was away at the time that the accidents happened, but he could have reprogrammed the computer before he left, couldn't he? It's possible that he wanted a good excuse to get rid of Charlie, isn't it? From what you've told me about your father being involved in Bret's company, I think that may be behind it."

Charlie did look stunned now. His face was going quite pale as he thought about it.

"But why get rid of *me*? Do you suppose he thought I knew something or heard something from my father? But I don't! Dad didn't seem to want to talk about business in the months before he died, so there's nothing I know that Bret could have worried about," he said, looking baffled.

"Remember when you accidentally locked into that information on the office computer?" said Dan. "Bret seemed to get real mad at you after that, I hear."

"Ye-es," said Charlie. "You're right, he did. He was more angry than I thought he would be, knowing it was an accident on my part," Charlie remembered. "And it *was* all data about Bret's companies – and my father's name was there, too. But what was it?"

Dan shook his head. "I don't know – but did your father ever use that computer? Could he have found something on it that Bret didn't want him to see, do you think? Or something about somebody else, for that matter? I'm also investigating a Maryland senator, a certain Mr William Gatti. He's involved in Bret's companies too, and he's beginning to look pretty shady."

"This is incredible," said Charlie, putting his head in his hands. "I know Bret is ambitious, ruthless even, but I never suspected he might go to criminal lengths to make money. I guess I've always thought he sailed close to the wind, and Dad even hinted at that, too, but this—"

"Look, Charlie," said Dan gently. "What I'm going to say next may come as a bit of shock to you, but here goes. Have you ever wondered if your father's accident was truly an accident? You see, I've got a hunch that he discovered too much about Bret's deals and—"

"No!" Charlie shot out of his chair. "That can't be true! Bret wouldn't sink to that level! *Murder?* I can't believe it!"

I got up quickly and went round the table to Charlie.

"I just hope you know what you're doing," I said to Dan. "You can't mess around with Charlie's feelings like this unless you're pretty sure that there's evidence to prove what you're saying."

I was shaking but trying to keep my voice calm, for Charlie's sake. I put my arm round his broad shoulders.

"I'm pretty sure I'm right," said Dan quietly. "I'm pretty sure Bret and Will Gatti have been manipulating the markets over certain shares so that they can make a huge profit – and then sell, fast, before the truth comes out and the shares plummet. From what I can discover, there's something big going to break at about the time of the Hunt Cup. Senator Gatti will be there, along with other prestigious folk, and my information is that that date is critical."

"I just can't believe it," said Charlie. He was pale, but in control, the awful truth beginning to sink in. "Does this mean Rick is involved, too? I knew he was despicable, but I wouldn't have thought he'd be involved in anything so dirty."

"I don't have any hard evidence yet, and I need it, fast," said Dan. "I'm not sure about Rick, I haven't found anything that ties him in to what Bret's doing yet, but you never know."

We were all so shocked at what Dan had told us that for a moment we couldn't think of anything to say. Dan got up from his chair, took another gulp of coffee and turned to Charlie.

"I'm sorry I had to do this, Charlie, but I'm gonna need your help. I know how you must feel about your father, but believe me, I'll do everything I can to find out the truth." He put his hand on Charlie's shoulder. "I know this'll be painful, but could you have a look around here, and see if your father left any notes on his business deals with Bret, or anything that might point us in the right direction?"

Charlie nodded. "I can do that," he said.

"Why didn't you tell us before, Dan?" I asked him. "You had every chance that night you followed me here. Why didn't you explain then?"

"I guess really I didn't want to put you both in any danger by revealing too much at that time," Dan said. "Can you understand? Especially when I began to think that Charlie's father hadn't died accidentally. I wanted to tell you, but I just thought it was too risky."

We had to believe him.

"I know I'm going to need your help," he said, looking at us both, "and I'm real sorry I have to rush away now, but I have to chase something up. I'll be in touch soon. Goodnight, Mr and Mrs Hunter-Davies, sorry about busting in like this. Goodnight, everyone, and thanks for the coffee."

After he left, there was silence in the kitchen.

"What everyone needs is some food," said Ned. "Then we'll talk about what Dan's told us – try and remember any details that might make things add up – and work out a plan. But food first!"

Good old Ned. He was always such a tower of strength in a crisis and he'd managed to break the tension at just the right moment and focus on what we should do next. And he was right – although none of us thought we'd be able to eat a thing, we managed large quantities of delicious roast lamb, new potatoes and ratatouille, followed by one of Sarah's apple tarts and cream.

Later, we sat round the fire in the beautiful living room, endlessly going over what Dan had told us and trying to work out what Bret could be up to.

"I never did like Bret King!" said Claudia violently, the flickering flames making her look even more golden than usual, and her eyes sparkling with a wicked glint. "I tell you,

Charlie, if what Dan Ricardo says is true, about Dick, I mean, I'll do anything to put that man behind bars – for a very long time! Now, to much nicer business – I'd adore you to ride Paddy for me in the Hunt Cup. Has Becky mentioned it?"

It was good to talk about something so familiar and real after all the speculation.

"She has, and I'd be happy to, Claudia," said Charlie, smiling at her. "I think Paddy's a terrific horse and he stands a good chance of doing real well now he's got over his desire to dump his rider!"

I glared at him in mock anger. But I was just happy that he felt he wanted to take part – after everything that had happened this evening, his life was looking pretty bleak.

Back at the Barn, my head was reeling, and not from my injury, either. The doctors had been very encouraging about that, and when I'd been allowed to look in a mirror for the first time at the hospital, my poor ear hadn't been as horrible as I'd imagined. My neck was still swollen and bruised down one side, but the stitches on the ear itself were neat. I had to hand it to them, they'd made a pretty good job of things! Now I only had to wear a large gauze dressing over the wound, but nothing too unsightly, and my hair covered most of it.

I lay in bed, still unable to take in everything that Dan had told us, and feeling tense and nervous. I just hoped that he would be able to get the evidence he needed. From what he'd told us, he had to try and prove that Bret (and probably the senator) were involved in a major real estate deal that was going to force the share price of Bret's company sky high. Then he'd sell and pull out – fast, before the share price took a nose-dive. It looked as though Dick had discovered the truth of what Bret was up to and somehow Dan had to find evidence of this to back up his theory, otherwise it looked as though Bret was going to get away with – I hardly dared even to *think* it – murder!

CHAPTER SEVENTEEN

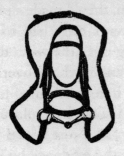

"It's the big day at last," said Kelly at breakfast-time, coming up to me in the kitchen.

"That's right," I said, "and I'm glad it's here. I can't stand the couple of days before a big race."

It was a relief to go with Kelly to the stable to check on Paddy and Grudie. Paddy greeted me with his head nodding, and I let myself into his stable before Kelly gave him the big grooming.

"Now listen, Paddy," I said, putting my face close to his neck, "you're not to dump Charlie, you hear me? Just be your normal, wonderful self." I gave him a final slap and left Kelly to sort him out.

I made my way down the now familiar

Barn to check on Grudie. Dave was with him in the stable but I was pleased that Grudie knew me well enough to signal his pleasure at my arrival by wiggling his ears backwards and forwards to show his excitement.

"How's he doing, Dave?" I asked.

"He's fine, Becky," said Dave. "Leg's all healed up and he's raring to go. It's just great that Mr King got Mike Huber lined up to ride him for the last couple of days. He's a real top-class jockey, Becky, you can be sure of that. The lads are all feeling relieved, I can tell you. Those accidents to the horses got them real upset – they didn't know what was going on or why."

"I know, Dave. It's been difficult for all of us. We'll just have to try and concentrate on the big race. Mike's really good – I read an article on him recently, he's the number one jockey over here, isn't he?"

Dave nodded. "He's going to take Grudie for a spin right now," he said. "He wants a chance to have a final chat with you beforehand, if that's OK."

"It's fine," I said, turning to the horse.

"Now, Grudie, none of your impetuous dashes, please," I said, looking him up and down over the half-door of the stable. He looked wonderful. Trim and fit and gleaming, his unusual chestnut colouring glowing in the light and his mane, with its flaxen streaks, already groomed and plaited. It's true he was no beauty, with his big, ugly head, long body and short legs, but you could almost feel his energy and enthusiasm. He was a great horse and he was definitely becoming one of my favourites.

I turned round as I heard footsteps coming up behind me, and I could feel my heart beginning to thump in my chest as I saw Bret approaching. He had Rick with him, and Mike Huber looked tiny beside them. Bret appeared tense and angry, and if I could have run away at that moment, I would have done.

"So, Rick's not good enough for Claudia's precious horse, eh? So much for loyalty to the Barn. I hear you're even letting that interfering Charlie Mann ride him," he said sarcastically to me.

I tried to explain. "I couldn't let Rick ride Paddy, he hasn't done enough riding recently, and he'd be too heavy – he wouldn't be able to slim down enough for the ride. And Paddy's Claudia's horse, Bret, and she really wanted Ch—"

"Don't bother explaining!" roared Bret. "I just hope you've made Mike here darn sure that he knows all Grudie's tricks. We can't have my horse losing today of all days. Is that clear?"

Rick was standing in the background, looking uneasy and embarrassed, not knowing where to put himself. "And you can make yourself useful, you no-good son of mine! Shows how much talent you've got if you can't even get a ride on the English horse! You've never been any good at anything – you're a born failure, just like your mother!"

I could feel my face turning scarlet – partly because I felt so angry with Bret for being so rude, and partly through embarrassment for Rick. How could his own father belittle him in front of everybody! What a horrible man!

Rick's face had gone from red to white as Bret continued to fling insults at him. Poor Rick, I was actually beginning to feel sorry for him.

Trying to clear the air, I turned to Mike. "Hi, Mike, can we have a few words about Grudie before you take him out for the last time?" I said, smiling at him.

"Sure," said Mike, clearly finding Bret's behaviour as embarrassing as everyone else. "Let's grab some coffee and we'll talk over a few things."

I led him over to the kitchen, talking as we went.

"I just want to tell you what we did yesterday, plus a bit more. The main thing to remember is that Grudie's a wonderful horse, he's got fantastic stamina and loyalty – once he commits himself, there's no turning back. And he's really big-hearted, so you can ask a lot from him."

"He's certainly highly-strung," said Mike, grinning.

"Well," I said, "that's one of the things I've been concentrating on, as I told you. The exercise programme's helped to make him more athletic, and he's calmed down a lot now he's more confident. He doesn't have any really bad habits, but he is impetuous, and he's fallen a couple of times – but he's certainly got guts!"

Then I led Mike through my plan for pacing the race: if Grudie took a strong hold about fifteen lengths away from the fence, he shouldn't fight him, just hold the contact and he would back off the fence himself. I also told him Grudie's little signals – how his bottom lip flapped up and down if he got over-anxious, and how his ears indicated his excitement. I was very pleased with Mike. He'd switched on to exactly what I was saying about Grudie over the past couple of days, and understood everything that I'd been trying to do with him.

I felt reassured that all my work wouldn't go for nothing, and I walked back over to my room to change. I needed to get my thoughts together before the race and think about whether there was anything else I should tell Mike – or Charlie, for that matter.

Just as I put my foot on the bottom step up to the lads' quarters, Dan appeared at my shoulder.

"Becky," he said urgently. "I'm real glad I've caught you before you leave for the race. I just want you to know that I'll be there, at the Hunt Cup. I'm pretty certain that things are going to break today. The share price in Bret's real estate company was higher yesterday than it's ever been, and it could be he's already sold out. We won't know till Monday morning. But I have to be at the race in case I can pick up on any information that could lead to an exposure."

I obviously looked shocked, because Dan put his hand on my shoulder. "Look, Becky," he said. "If you discover anything, *anything* at all about Bret, find me. I'll be around the main enclosure, I guess."

I could see he was beginning to feel desperate.

"I'll keep my eyes open, Dan," I promised him.

We looked at each other briefly, and then Dan was gone, giving my shoulder a final firm grip. Somehow, although I felt frightened and tense with all this as well as the race to think about, I could feel a strong sense of determination developing inside me. I really would do anything to help Charlie find out the truth behind his father's car accident, and what Bret was up to. As I ran up the steps, I even felt eager to get to the course, and see for myself if there was anything I could discover.

As I pushed open the door of my room, I saw two huge, shiny bags sitting on my bed. They looked expensive, and I guessed immediately who they were from. It had to be Claudia! Her sense of timing was immaculate.

I found a note pinned to each bag. The first one was from Claudia:

> *Becky, darling –*
> *I knew you needed some extra*
> *courage. This should do the trick!*
> *Remember, The Hunt Cup is one*
> *big fashion parade.*
> *Hugs and kisses,*
> *Claudia.*

The second envelope had a note from Pammy inside:

> *Becky –*
> *Knock 'em dead! See you there!*
> *Pammy*

I smiled to myself. It was typical of both of them and showed just how generous and spontaneous they were. But how would I choose?

I started to open Claudia's bag, feeling the expensive rustle of tissue paper. I pulled out a soft grey and white polka-dot silk dress and, nestling underneath it, a fine black straw hat with a turned-up brim. Underneath that was a pair of black and white high-heeled shoes. Wow, I breathed. Chic and expensive, like Claudia herself.

I wrenched open Pammy's bag (I recognised the name of the store from our shopping trip together) and took out a tiny puce mini skirt and a black hat, slightly wacky, with a brim turned up in the front. It had an amazing flower sewn on it, which added a touch of startling colour. Quite restrained for Pammy, but what was I going to do? How could I avoid upsetting one of them?

In the end, I opted for Claudia's dress and Pammy's hat, and hoped I looked OK. As I brushed out my hair ready to leave, put the hat on my head and stuck one of my tiny, diamond stud earrings that had been my mother's into my good ear, I glanced at myself in the mirror. Not bad, though I did say it myself! I hoped Charlie would think so too.

The clothes had provided a welcome break from worrying about the race, but now I had to face the world. I felt nervous thinking about what Dan had told me, and how he thought something big was due to happen at the Hunt Cup. But I felt determined to try and find the evidence needed to expose Bret if I could – but what was it, and where? I didn't have time to look at the computer again, and even if I did, what was the name of the file that Charlie had typed in by accident? Without that information, on an unfamiliar machine, I could have been trying to find it for at least a couple of hours.

I ran down the stairs into the yard, where Grudie and Paddy were already in the huge transporter, waiting to go. Kelly and Dave were coming with us and Scott was driving. Bret and Rick were to follow later. The other lads were standing round, ready to wish us luck.

"Thanks, everyone," I said, quite overcome, as the lads started clapping and saying, "Wow!" and "Good luck, Becky, you can do it!" Americans have a particular way of whooping that the English just can't do without sounding ridiculous.

One of the lads helped me up into the cab of the transporter, and we were off!

CHAPTER EIGHTEEN

As we got nearer the course, I began to feel the excitement that always surrounds a major race. We were in a queue of luxurious transporters like ours, and there were limousines stretching as far as the eye could see! The Maryland spring weather had done its stuff and the sun was shining down on the crowd, which was beginning to buzz with anticipation.

I could see what Claudia meant about one big fashion parade! Everyone looked very stylish and there was more of an air of the Derby about this race than any of the others I'd been to before. Huge marquees had been set up for entertaining and large groups of elegant people were spread about under the trees where there were picnic tables and chairs.

Scott drove the transporter carefully to its allocated site and relief flooded through me as I saw Charlie, already kitted out in Claudia's familiar blue and yellow colours, waiting for our arrival. He looked stunning! His tanned face and blond hair gleamed and his tall, lithe figure was shown at its best in the breeches and boots that jockeys wear.

"Charlie!" I said, jumping down into the arms which were held out to help me.

"Hi, Becky," he said, smiling at me, and somehow I could tell he thought I looked OK. "Everything all right?"

"Paddy and Grudie are fine, they're being spoilt rotten by Karen and Dave. Can we go and walk the course? There are some things we need to talk about – and Mike can come with us."

The three of us – me with boots on which I'd temporarily swapped for my high heels – started to walk the course. The fences seemed massive, towering above us as we walked up to inspect them. I just hoped Paddy would manage over the really big, five-bar jumps.

We talked about the going and where it

would be best to run the horses – Grudie always liked to be out in front, but Paddy preferred to run about second or third and make a headlong dash at the end. Mike looked even smaller next to the huge timber rails, and I was struck by the sheer guts that successful jockeys needed.

As we finished our inspection, Mike went off to get saddled up and Charlie and I turned to each other.

"Good luck, Charlie," I whispered, looking straight into his eyes. "I hope Paddy behaves himself." And I reached up to give him a kiss. As I did so, my eye was caught by a St Christopher medal hanging round his neck.

"What's this?" I asked him, smiling, "I haven't seen you wearing it before."

"No," said Charlie, suddenly looking wistful. "My father gave it to me to wear on my first Hunt Cup race – just for luck."

I put my hand up to touch it, as though it was a lucky talisman, a link with Dick, and turned it over in my fingers.

"What's this written on the back?" I asked.

"I didn't realise there was anything on the

back. In fact, I'm sure there wasn't when Dad first gave it to me," said Charlie, looking puzzled. He looked at the inscription and read it aloud: *"File = NOH TRF."*

I gasped, realisation flooding through me. "These letters, Charlie! I recognise them! I'm sure I do! They're the ones that you accidentally punched into the computer! Remember when you got into that file of Bret's real estate deals? Your fingers slipped on to the wrong keys, so you typed NOH TRF instead of BIG RED, the name of one of Bret's horses! And here they are again, see? NOH TRF!"

For a moment, neither of us could speak or quite believe what we saw.

Suddenly, I knew that this must be it! This must be the evidence we needed to help Dan expose Bret. Dick had given Charlie this key to the shady business that he suspected Bret was involved in. He must have realised that this would be the one safe way of communicating the information. Perhaps he'd even had a fear that his own life would be in danger, and that by the time Charlie read the new inscription, he wouldn't be alive. I shuddered.

I grabbed Charlie's arm. "Dan was right! Listen, he told me he'd be here and that I should find him if I discovered any information about Bret. Charlie, find Dan and tell him to meet me in – in—" where? – "in the winner's enclosure! I'm going to get that file we locked into printed out. I'm sure that's the information Dan needs to expose Bret!"

And before Charlie could say anything, I was off, running as fast as I could, and thankful that I'd put on my riding boots. Poor Charlie was left staring after me. Now I had to find Pammy, fast!

I didn't know what she would be wearing, but I knew it would be eye-catching, and I ran, ducking and weaving through the elegant crowds, towards the hospitality tents. There, talking vivaciously to a cool young guy with dark hair and olive skin, stood Pammy. She was wearing her favourite lime green which had helped me to spot her, and I ran up to her, panting and gasping for breath, and grabbing her arm. I turned her round to face me.

"Pammy... sorry... come... now!" She got the message. Evidently, Claudia and Ned had filled her in on our night at Charlie's, and she'd been expecting some excitement. Together, we ran, almost knocking people over in the elegant crowd, towards the car park and Pammy's sports car.

"We have to get to the Barn, fast!" I gulped, as we ran up to her car, leaning on it and trying to catch our breath.

"Well, jump right in, then," said Pammy. And she flung her little bag into the back, leapt into the driver's seat and started the engine with a roar. I slid in beside her, grateful to be sitting down, my injured ear beginning to throb in an unpleasant way.

Pammy negotiated the cars and wound her way skilfully to the exit. She waved and grinned flamboyantly at the guard on the gate as we shot through, swerving to avoid a passing limo.

"Pammy, let me explain," I said, turning to look at her as she drove dangerously fast towards the Barn. "We need to go to the office and punch in the code that Charlie discovered accidentally the other day. We flashed up a load of details about Bret's latest real estate deal, and he got very angry and jumpy about it when he discovered we'd seen it. We just thought he was angry at Charlie being careless, but now we know better! He obviously thought we'd understood the information we'd seen. Pammy, I'm *sure* now that that must be the details of the deal that Bret and the Senator are putting together – the stuff that Dan Ricardo told us about!"

"Hang on in there, babe!" said Pammy, "I'll get you there just as fast as I can!"

After a nightmare journey which seemed to flash past in a blur of squealing tyres and flashing lights, we made it to the Barn. I flung myself out of the car, and went straight towards the office, ignoring the few lads who were working. I must have looked half demented, my silk dress hitched high up my legs after the car ride and my boots making an odd contrast with my wacky black hat! I don't know why I'd been clutching it on my head – people do funny things in panic.

Luckily, with the lads still about, the office was unlocked and I dropped into the chair by the computer, gasping for breath, with Pammy coming up behind me. The computer flashed into life and I typed in NOH TRF. Shaking, I watched the file materialise on screen. Here it was again! All those details! I quickly realised that it was a list of shares in something called The Bear Island Resort Project, together with all the names of the investors. Glancing at it quickly, I could see that the share price was beginning to go through the roof, and that the last entry had been made only yesterday! Today's date leapt out at me – it was the day for The Bear Island Resort Project to be finalised. I yelled at Pammy to turn on the printer, clicked on *Print-All*, and held my breath.

The computer whirred into action and the printer began disgorging the information.

"We have to get back to the racecourse just as soon as this has printed out," I gasped, turning to Pammy.

"You thought we were fast coming over, you should see what's going to happen going back," she said, grinning. You could always rely on Pammy in a crisis!

As the printer beeped, signalling the end of the run, I grabbed up the papers and started to run out of the office, with Pammy close behind me.

"Can't stop to explain!" I yelled at the lads. "Tell you later!" And Pammy and I jumped into the car, drove like lightning through the Barn and down the drive again. The guard was curious. He hadn't opened the gate when he'd seen us, this time, so we had to slow down, signalling frantically for him to open up.

"Hey, ladies!" he called. "What's the big hurry?"

"Would you just get that gate open?" called out Pammy, waving her sunglasses at him furiously. "And no questions! Catch you later," she called airily, as we squealed our way out of the gate and swerved into the road outside.

Talk about speed! Pammy's foot must have nearly gone through the floor, we were going so fast.

Eventually, my head dizzy with images of fields and houses we'd flashed past, I saw the familiar racecourse looming up ahead. The marquees and crowds all seemed very remote, as though normal life was carrying on just out of reach. We began to slow down for the gateway.

I tried to shout at Pammy above the noise of the engine. "Pammy, as soon as we get there, I'll jump out and you ring the police on your car phone, tell them to get here, quick!"

"No need," said Pammy, smiling wryly. "I think they're here already."

We heard the whine of the police siren closing in on us and I leapt out of the car and started running towards the racecourse, the vital papers clutched in my hand. I hoped that Pammy would know what to say to the police before they dragged her off to the station for speeding!

I couldn't see anyone now I needed them – no Ned or Claudia, no Dan or anyone, and I stopped, trying to catch my breath. The crowd seemed to be roaring its lungs out, so the race must be nearly over. I had to get to the winner's enclosure – Dan was bound to be there, I thought desperately.

At last I reached the white rails fencing off the enclosure – and there was Bret! He was standing with Senator William Gatti, one on either side of a table holding the Cup. Grudie must have won! Just for a moment, I forgot all the nasty things that were happening as I sensed a feeling of pure elation at the thought of Grudie winning, and all my hard work with him paying off. You wonderful horse! I thought to myself.

Something brought me back to my senses again with a bump. I spotted Dan, hovering nervously behind Bret. I ran towards the gate of the enclosure, but was stopped by the guard on the entrance.

"Sorry, ma'am," she said. "Can I see your owner's ticket, please?"

"Ticket?" I asked, bewildered. But of course I'd lost it. Somewhere in the rush of the last hour, I'd dropped it – it had been pinned to my dress. I couldn't believe it!

And there was Grudie, being led into the enclosure by Dave, and Mike was dismounting, and Bret was about to be presented with the Cup by the senator.

Bret was looking up at the sky. Following his gaze, I saw, very high up, a helicopter, and as soon as I saw it, I could just hear the whirr of its engine.

Bret and the senator were both looking distracted as the noise of the helicopter grew louder. Could it be for their getaway? It must be!

I was desperate: I screamed. I screamed so loudly that Dan saw me, which is what I'd wanted.

"Dan! Dan!" I yelled, waving the pieces of paper frantically in the air.

He ran across and grabbed my arm and before I knew what was happening, he'd pulled me through the enclosure entrance, past the startled guard and into the ring, where he snatched the papers from my hand and began to read them anxiously.

"This is it!" he gasped. "This is everything I need, right here!" And without waiting to explain anything further, he turned and ran across to the microphone, grabbing it from the hands of the senator.

"*Ladies and Gentlemen*!" his voice crackled over the PA system. "*You may wonder what I'm doing here. My name is Dan Ricardo and I'm an investigative reporter on the* Herald Tribune. "

The crowd was looking confused and people were muttering to each other. Bret and the senator looked stunned, waiting to see what Dan was talking about. The helicopter whirred very low overhead and began to make its descent over the racecourse.

Suddenly, Dan realised what was going to happen and started to speak more quickly. *"I'm here to tell you that these two gentlemen, Mr Bret King and Senator William Gatti, are both involved in a business scam that's going to mean that a lot of you good people right here are going to be in trouble. You've heard of The Bear Island Resort Project, well—"*

Several people in the crowd gasped and there was a movement towards the winner's enclosure. The noise of the helicopter grew louder as it hovered metres above the racecourse.

Dan struggled to make himself heard. *"Please!"* he said. *"Listen to me! These men have been forcing up the share price just so they can sell at the top of the market and make millions. Then the shares will crash and—"*

Bret and the senator leapt into action. It was like something out of a Hollywood movie. They started to make a run for it, shoving past me and pushing through the crowd surrounding the enclosure. I stood like an idiot, not knowing what to do.

"*Becky*!" yelled Dan on the microphone. "*Call the police, get after them!*"

That got me going. I turned and followed Bret, just able to see his red head over the top of the crowds which parted as he and Senator Gatti stumbled towards the waiting helicopter.

I heard people gasping as I passed.

"Bret *King*, Will *Gatti* – I don't believe it!"

"Oh dear heavens – didn't we have money in that deal?"

I pushed my way through them, with Dan hot on my heels, reaching the rails that ran round the racecourse just in time to see Bret in the distance, lumbering towards the helicopter. The senator seemed to have tripped halfway there, and was surrounded by a group of stewards as he lay on the ground.

I couldn't believe it! Bret was going to get away with it! He was nearly at the helicopter!

Then, as I ducked under the rails and started to run towards him – I hadn't got a clue what I was going to do if I did reach him – I saw Ned. He seemed to appear out of nowhere, looking extremely agile for someone his age, and did a flying tackle around Bret's legs. Of course! I thought. Ned's SAS training!

Then beside me, clutching her wide-brimmed hat to her head but still managing to look devastating, was Claudia.

"My English hero!" she breathed, gazing at where Ned lay on top of Bret King.

After that, everyone appeared. Charlie and Dan, and the police and Pammy, all of them flooding on to the racecourse. Ned had got Bret's arm up behind his back and was sitting on him when the police arrived. Though not completely sure yet of the exact nature of Bret's crime, the police had him in their grip as they led him and the senator towards their waiting cars.

Pammy strolled towards me, as cool as a cucumber. I was standing between Charlie and Dan, watching in horror at the scene that had unfolded in front of us.

"It just took me a little time to persuade them I was telling the truth, that's all," she said, swinging her little bag, and looking pleased with herself. "But timing is everything," she said nonchalantly.

"Oh, Pammy," I giggled, "you are truly fantastic!"

I leant against Charlie's shoulder, exhausted by all the running and chasing, my knees beginning to tremble in a most unladylike way. Charlie put his arm round me.

"Well done, Becky," he said, turning me to face him. "You were great, and so was Dan," he said, looking at him.

"Just in the nick of time!" said Dan. His dark hair was ruffled and his tie was hanging loosely round his neck. He really looked quite cute.

"I have to go with the police now," he said to me, "to give them all the evidence I have. And Charlie," he added, more seriously, "I talked with them this morning about all this, which is how they got here so quickly. I must tell you that they're now going to re-open the file on your father's accident. I know it'll be painful for you, but at least you'll know the truth."

He moved away, then turned to look back at us all. "So long. I'll be seeing you guys." He raised his hand in farewell and followed the police to their waiting cars.

"He's a nice guy," said Charlie.

"Yes," I said, "really nice!"

"But not too nice, I hope," he said, looking into my eyes.

Ned and Claudia were walking towards us across the racecourse where Ned had been talking to one of the police officers taking charge of the helicopter pilot.

"Ned!" I said, running to him, "you were brilliant! I promise I won't make any more jokes about OAPs."

He grabbed the back of my neck in mock rage and pulled me towards him.

"If you weren't my own dear granddaughter, I'd strangle you with my bare hands," he said, laughing.

"Come on, you two," said Claudia. "You sure know how to make a girl feel left out."

And she laughed her throaty laugh.

So Ned, Claudia, Pammy, Charlie and I all linked arms and turned back towards the crowds who were beginning to disperse – this was one Hunt Cup they'd never forget.

Charlie and I had broken away from Ned and Claudia, and Pammy had gone over to chat to the tall, dark, handsome young man again, when we noticed Rick. I have to admit, I'd forgotten all about him in the drama. He stood a little way off, looking lost and rather frightened.

Charlie put his hand on my arm. "Wait here, Becky," he said. After some minutes of talking and gesticulating, I saw Charlie put his arm round Rick's shoulders and lead him back towards me.

It was a touching sight, I have to admit. Although I thought Rick was unpleasant and slimy, no one deserved a father like Bret, and when I'd witnessed how his father had treated him earlier that day, I'd started to feel sorry for him.

"Becky," said Charlie, as they reached me,

"Rick knew nothing. He swears that it was nothing to do with him, the accidents to the horses and everything. And I have to believe him. It looks like Bret was tampering with the programmes just so he would have the excuse to fire me. The police have told him that they're looking into my father's death again, too."

"I want to explain too, Becky," said Rick. "Dad never let me near his interesting business deals. Sure, he wanted me to go into the real estate business – but I never wanted to. My heart was always set on being an amateur jockey and helping train the horses. But Dad never thought I was capable of doing anything right! And I know I'm kind of bitter about my leg and not being able to ride as well as I used to, but I would never actually harm Charlie – most of my life I've tried to be *like* him – and Dick was like an uncle to me. Now I guess Charlie hates me – who can blame him – and you too, probably."

"Look, Rick," I said, trying to sound positive. "You haven't been the nicest person in the world, but why don't we try and work together for the last couple of weeks that I'm still here? And I'm sure both you and Charlie need a friend at the moment. What do you say to a fresh start?"

They both let out a long sigh of relief. Rick smiled tentatively at Charlie – I'd obviously said the right thing.

"Sure, Rick," said Charlie. "Maybe we can make a new start together. Who knows how long Bret will be away, and there's a lot of things to find out about my father's accident. But if you're prepared to give it a go, we could work together at the Barn, keep things running with Max? No more lying or snide remarks, OK?"

"OK," said Rick, nodding, and somehow I thought he'd try and make a go of things now. He really valued Charlie's friendship, I was sure of that.

The thought of Charlie and Rick working at the Barn together made me feel left out. Was this a place where I could make a life for myself, too? I wondered.

✕

CHAPTER NINETEEN

Ned, Claudia, Pammy, and I all went over to Charlie's place to have some supper and unwind. Rick was at the police station, trying to find out what Bret was being charged with, and he didn't manage to call us till late.

Kelly and Dave were over the moon – Grudie had won, and Paddy (I'd been so crazy trying to nail Bret that I hadn't even asked Charlie where they'd come in the Cup) had come in third. I was more thrilled about these two things than I could possibly have imagined when I'd first arrived out here.

Charlie told me on the way back that Paddy had gone really steadily. He'd taken the timber fences with all the courage and strength that I knew he had. He wasn't as agile as

Grudie, but he was equally big-hearted, and he and Charlie had thoroughly enjoyed the race.

Mike, when at last I'd found him at the course, told me that Grudie had been a horse in a million. He was controlled, fast and amazingly athletic, and he hadn't let his impetuous nature get the better of him this time.

"You did one helluva job on that horse, Becky," he said to me.

I must admit, after the tension of the day and the running around, I could feel tears beginning to well up in my eyes. I gulped and said, "Thanks, Mike, I appreciate you saying that." But I had to turn away quickly so that he couldn't see what a baby I was!

Claudia was so pleased with Paddy that she was threatening to keep him out here permanently, so that he could become a real American champion. I'm not sure what I feel about that, but I've certainly got mixed feelings about the thought of both of us going home.

Later in the evening, Rick did telephone us. He sounded exhausted – drained by all the things he'd learnt about Bret. Even if Bret was a monster, he was still his father.

Rick explained The Bear Island Resort Project to us. Apparently, Bret owned five hundred acres of land along a beautiful lake. He'd developed a plan to build a luxury resort – with a golf course, tennis courts, holiday houses and a health club. But the site was protected by an environmental agency as a place of outstanding natural beauty and wildlife.

Bret had been trying to bribe and blackmail the planners and state licensors to get permission for his development. That's when Dick had realised that Bret was up to no good. He found out that a report was shortly to be published saying that planning would *not* be given. Bret, on the other hand, was telling his backers, secretly, that he'd definitely been told that planning permission *would* be given.

He'd convinced his backers to invest millions of dollars and had planned that, just as the shares reached an all-time high, he would sell. Bret knew that the report was to be published on the Monday after the Hunt Cup, so he had to sell his shares the Friday before and make his escape, fast. He'd wanted to win the Hunt Cup, and all the prestige that went with it, so badly that he'd risked leaving his escape till the last minute.

Bret had bribed Senator Will Gatti into lobbying the planners and, in turn, bribing them to agree to the Bear Island Resort Project. The senator had also invested thousands of dollars with Bret. It was clear now that they were both set to have made a fortune and would have got away with it if we hadn't foiled them at the last minute.

Rick told us that Dan was down at the police station too and was busy putting his exclusive together for his national newspaper. Dan deserved his by-line – it was because of him that Bret and the senator had been caught. With a little help from Pammy and me, of course!

By the time I got back to the Barn that night and talked to the lads, it was very late. Of course I stopped on my way up to bed to say goodnight to my two stars, Paddy and Grudie! Paddy was the other side of his stable, but as soon as he heard my footsteps, he whinnied and came to the door straight away. I know I'm soppy about horses, but I'm convinced he looked very pleased with himself! He was tired but satisfied, and he nudged me with his big head as I stroked his neck and ran my fingers down the middle of his nose, scratching it in the way he liked.

"You were fantastic, Paddy," I whispered to him. "You're the best advertisement for British horses, you know that? You're an absolute star."

If anyone had heard me, they would probably have thought I was mad, but I didn't care. Paddy *was* a star and I loved him best in all the world – after Red Rag (or Monkey, as I called him, back at home), and now there was Grudie, too.

I said goodnight to Paddy and walked down to Grudie's stable. Dave was still there, leaning over the door in the semi-darkness. I think he was doing a bit of horse-worshipping, too.

"He is wonderful, isn't he?" I murmured, coming up behind Dave. "You've all been brilliant today, well done."

"He sure is," said Dave. "And thanks to you, Becky, he's been cured of his naughty habits. He's one of the finest horses in America now."

"You may be right," I agreed. "Goodnight, Grudie, you champion!" I said as I rubbed his head. "And Dave, I hope your dreams come true. Goodnight, and thanks."

I walked slowly through the peaceful Barn, taking time to notice all the wonderful things about it again. Its gleaming wood and immaculate floor – and everything in its right place. I strolled on, thinking about the day and looking forward to a good night's sleep. With just a little dream about Charlie, maybe?

But there was one thing I had to do before I went to bed, and that was write to Jamie. I just had to let him know what had happened.

> *Dear Jamie*
> *You'll never guess! Grudie won the*
> *Hunt Cup and Paddy came in*
> *third! Charlie rode a brilliant race*
> *and Paddy's looking very pleased*

with himself. Grudie's really a horse in a million.

Jamie, I have to tell you something. Bret King's been arrested for dirty dealing in some real estate project. We had a wild time at The Hunt Cup, and we found the evidence against him just in time. You'd never believe how Hollywood it all was with a helicopter landing on the racecourse and police chases, and Ned was a star! He tackled Bret and stopped him making his escape.

Jamie, I'm babbling on, in my usual way, but what I want to say is that I'm seriously thinking of staying on – I really feel I could do just about anything, anywhere, right now. America, the world? Who knows? But I wanted to let you know – being over here has made me realise I'm not ready to settle down in Ben and Sue's stables just yet, even though I might want

to later on. I'm confused, Jamie,
and I feel very far away from you.
Write soon.
Hugs and kisses, Becky.

The truth was, I was thinking rather a lot about Charlie – I just couldn't seem to get him out of my mind.

EPILOGUE

Now here I am, sitting in the sunshine on the white post-and-rails fence at Bret King's Barn. My thoughts are beginning to fall into place as the warmth of the sun seeps through my shirt and into my body. I feel invigorated, just like Grudie and Paddy, who've been let out to play on the lush spring grass. Their coats are shining and they look wonderful.

Behind me, standing in the middle of the yard, Charlie and Rick are chatting to all the lads, giving them their orders for the rest of the day. Everything is back to normal – only better. Rick is really making an effort and the shock of what Bret has done has somehow made him a nicer person. He and Charlie are organising the Barn and since the Hunt Cup, new clients have put their horses into the stables, even though some of them are the very people who Bret tried to swindle.

But they feel sympathetic towards Rick, and they were all friends of Dick's. That's why they want to support Charlie. And of course, Claudia has helped things along in her usual way. She's made a point of telling all her influential Maryland friends that Charlie is the best trainer around, along with her new granddaughter, of course! Grudie winning the Hunt Cup really put the Barn on the map, though.

Lost in thought, I didn't hear Charlie coming up behind me.

"Watching your favourite horses?" he said, standing very close to me.

I turned on the fence and found myself looking directly into his blue eyes. He moved a strand of hair away from my face, very tenderly, and my stomach did a huge lurch.

"I was just thinking about going home... what to do next... you know," I stammered. "I sort of feel the world's my oyster right now."

"And that's how it should be," said Charlie. "But I've got some ideas of my own. Want to hear them?"

He'd put his hands on my waist and, to be honest, I could hardly breathe, let alone speak. So I nodded.

"I've been wondering whether you'd be interested in training a couple of horses over in

Ireland. It's something Dick and I always wanted to do. I've talked to Rick about it as well, and he thinks it makes great business sense – spread the King name around the racing world. He's really not bad at business. Let's hope he sticks to the straight and narrow, though," he added wryly.

"Well... " I said, stupidly. "Yes... maybe... I don't really know... " I ended lamely.

Charlie came even closer, put his arms right round me and kissed me. "Maybe this will make up your mind?" he said.

I was smiling at him, still unable to speak, when I felt a strong nudge in my back. It was Paddy! He and Grudie were standing either side of me, inquisitive and excited. Paddy tossed his head up and down, as he often did, and Grudie waggled his ears.

"I think that's your answer!" I whispered to Charlie, laughing into his blue eyes.

Ginny Elliot
WINNING!

**Becky's trained a winner, but someone
wants her to lose...**

Becky is determined to be a top trainer
after she leaves school. She knows the
new chestnut steeplechaser has the
makings of a champion and Red Rag's
racing career gets off to a flying start!
Better still, in Becky's view, hunky
jockey Jamie Howland is riding him! But
someone is out to nobble Red Rag.
Becky is smart; she's worked out *how*,
but dare she discover who and why?

A cracking thriller by one of the most
accomplished riders in the world today.

0 00 675036 2
£3.99

Collins
An *Imprint* of HarperCollins*Publishers*

Ginny Elliot
RACE AGAINST TIME

**Becky faces her most important race ever
– to save Red Rag from a deadly virus!**

If Red Rag is to survive and if the new
wonderhorse, Paddy, is to win the
Grand National, Becky must discover
who is spreading the fatal horse virus
– and why. Will she trace the instigator
of the vicious blackmail threats? Why is
Tomas, the new jockey, behaving so
suspiciously? Is even her adored Jamie
truly trustworthy?

Another thrilling novel by this
internationally renowned rider set in the
exciting world of professional racing.

0 00 675163 6
£3.99

Collins
An *Imprint* of HarperCollins*Publishers*

Order Form

To order direct from the publishers, just make a list of the titles you want and fill in the form below:

Name

....

Address

....

....

....

Send to: Dept 6, HarperCollins Publishers Ltd, Westerhill Road, Bishopbriggs, Glasgow G64 2QT.

Please enclose a cheque or postal order to the value of the cover price, plus:

UK & BFPO: Add £1.00 for the first book, and 25p per copy for each additional book ordered.

Overseas and Eire: Add £2.95 service charge. Books will be sent by surface mail but quotes for airmail despatch will be given on request.

A 24-hour telephone ordering service is available to Visa and Access card holders: 0141- 772 2281

Collins
An *Imprint* of HarperCollins*Publishers*